I0531469

Shared Madness

Rick Moskovitz

FLUKE TALE PRODUCTIONS

Book Cover Design by The Book Cover Whisperer: ProfessionalBookCoverDesign.com

FLUKE TALE PRODUCTIONS

Shared Madness

Table of Contents

Most men are within a finger's breadth of being mad

Diogenes

Today I felt pass over me a breath of wind from the wings of madness

Charles Baudelaire

Preface

As a psychiatrist, I often struggled with competing ethical and legal responsibilities. In the course of providing treatment to relieve distress, I was expected to keep whatever my patients told me strictly confidential. At the same time, I was entrusted with preventing harm. Some patients posed the risk of harm to themselves, some of harm to others, and still others offered information about people around them who posed danger to them or to others. The responsibility to prevent harm was further complicated by my limited influence upon my patients' fates.

For the benefit of my trainees while I was teaching psychotherapy, I coined the "168 hour rule." Therapists typically spend an hour a week with their patients, helping them to understand how their thoughts and behavior influence their emotions and the course of their lives. During the remaining 167 hours, they are subject to the influence of others around them, of the media they consume, of the slings and arrows or ordinary life, and of their own impulses, any of which can screw up their lives in a heartbeat. And still, the doctor may be held responsible for bad outcomes, particularly if they occur by their patient's hand.

Balancing the duty to maintain confidentiality with the duty to prevent harm and walking the often fine line between them caused me many a sleepless night. And the severity of the dilemma was directly related to the magnitude of potential harm that I envisioned.

The seeds of **Shared Madness**, originally titled **Folie à Deux**, arose out of this ever-present burden and the aftermath of the attack on the World Trade Center on 9/11/2001. What if, I imagined, a patient were to share with me information about a possible future terrorist attack? And what if this information was shrouded in sufficient doubt that the consequences of withholding it weren't clear or compelling? Would the potential magnitude of an unlikely event be enough to breach the confidence of a patient and perhaps even put that patient in legal or physical jeopardy?

I framed my story against a backdrop of a psychotic patient who heard voices and experienced delusions of persecution that altered his perception of reality. What might a psychiatrist believe about a tale of treachery told by someone with such an unreliable and distorted view of his world? And it occurred to me that if the doctor was also hallucinating and delusional, assessing the validity of the threat would become even more daunting.

I wrote a half dozen chapters starting in 2005 along with some character backstories, got stuck, and filed it away while I continued to practice psychiatry. After retirement from practice, I turned again to writing, veering into science fiction, and completed the **Brink of Life Trilogy** in fits and starts over much of the past decade. The blank canvas of the future fed my imagination and the stories began to flow with increasing ease.

Last year, I stumbled upon the nearly forgotten file of **Folie a Deux**. Having drawn my trilogy to a close and honed my storytelling craft, I embraced the project with new confidence. And I brought to the task a new perspective, venturing into the first person, writing entirely through the eyes of my protagonist, and balancing the constraint of that limited perspective with the freedom of living in my character's head and experiencing his world fully. The story grew organically, expanding beyond its original framework into a full blown thriller.

I invite you now into Zack Tripler's world, filled with doubt and more than a touch of madness as he grapples with a life and death puzzle and seeks to recover his sanity.

Rick Moskovitz
June 2020

1

HOW DEAR the price of an unasked for kiss?

"You can't do this to me. Let me go. It's much too dangerous for me to be here."

Youssef glared at me with bloodshot eyes, deep set beneath thick black eyebrows that nearly met n the middle. His olive skin was darkened by several days of stubble. He wore black dress pants and a white button down shirt that was wrinkled and grimy. My eyes moved from the cuts and abrasions that covered his hands to the dirt packed under his fingernails.

"Please, Youssef," sobbed the dark skinned woman from across the room, "You're sick. You need help. Please talk to the doctor."

"This is your fault," he snapped back, pointing a grimy finger at the now cowering woman. "You had me brought here. Now you've put us both in danger."

He clutched a laptop computer tightly to his body with his ragged hands. The aides had tried to take it when they admitted him, but he wouldn't surrender it. They decided that it wasn't worth the battle and let him keep it.

"What danger?" I asked, looking for some way to engage him.

"What danger?" he echoed, rising suddenly to his feet. "How do I know that you're not one of them?"

I resisted the temptation to stand in response to his threatening posture. It was best not to challenge a frightened patient.

"Them?"

He opened his mouth as if to speak, but fell silent and sank back into his chair, the laptop still clutched to his chest.

"He hasn't slept in days," said the woman, who identified herself as his wife. "He's been hiding out in the woods, with a gun, from God knows who. He's been having terrible headaches and I think he's been hearing voices. He thinks someone's trying to kill him."

"Shut up! You've told him too much already. You'll get us both killed."

"Please help him doctor. He's not himself. He's always been so gentle. I don't know what's gotten into him."

When the aides came to take Youssef to his room, he went without a struggle. I wrote orders for close observation and olanzapine, an antipsychotic medication that I hoped would curb the terror and quell the voices that tormented him. Getting him to let down his guard enough to sleep would be the first hurdle in his treatment.

Youssef Al Saud had been brought to the hospital by Sheriff's deputies for emergency psychiatric evaluation. Despite being armed, he'd surrendered without a fight and had given up his weapon upon command. He hadn't volunteered anything about why he was hiding in the woods and responded to the officers' questions with stony silence.

According to his driver's license, he was 34 years old, but little other information about him had been available when he arrived at the hospital. The deputies had tracked down his wife from the address on his license and she'd arrived while he was being admitted. When Youssef did begin to speak, his English was fluent, but accented in a rhythm I took to be Middle Eastern in keeping with his name.

The next time I saw Youssef, he was dressed in clean hospital scrubs. He was freshly showered, but still unshaven, and his long, black hair was slicked straight back, still wet. The larger cuts on his hands had been dressed with Band-Aids. Traces of dirt were still visible under his fingernails. He sat across from me in the small consultation room, sipping coffee from a Styrofoam cup.

"How are you feeling this morning?" I asked.

"Groggy. Drugged. What the hell did you give me?" His speech was now slurred, but without any trace of the accent from our first encounter.

"A tranquilizer. To calm you down and help you sleep. You were very agitated last night."

"Agitated," he repeated, shaking his head, then scowling from beneath the dark eyebrows. "Why the hell wouldn't I be? Wouldn't you be agitated if the police tackled you, handcuffed you and brought you to some

God forsaken lockup without any defenses against your enemies?"

"What enemies?"

"No. I've said too much already." The coffee cup in his hand was shaking. He set it down on the table beside him. "What have you done with my laptop?"

"We sent it home with your wife. It'll be safer with her than here."

His olive skin turned ashen as he shot to his feet. "You idiot. You have no idea what you've done," he screamed, taking a step toward me. "You've endangered my whole family. I must get it back. I must get out of here right now." He moved toward the door and began to open it.

"You can't leave yet. You need treatment."

"Treatment for what? You think I'm crazy?"

"You've been running around in the woods with a gun. You've been hearing voices. You're not thinking clearly."

"And drugging me is going to make me think clearly? You're playing right into their hands. They want me weak and defenseless. You're helping them kill me." His words were now slow and deliberate. He looked outside the door of the room and saw the burly orderly standing just outside. After sizing up the situation, he let go of the door and sat back down.

"Look," he said, making direct eye contact, "I know what this must look like. You're just doing your job. I'll make you a deal. I'll stay a few days so you can see I'm not a maniac, but no more drugs. And I need to get my computer back before they find it. I need it here with me."

"I think you're going to need medication, but we can talk more about that later. If you cooperate, I won't force you to take anything without your consent. I'll see what we can do about getting you your computer tomorrow."

"No, not tomorrow." He wagged a single finger in front of his face. "Tomorrow will be too late. You must let me call my wife this morning. That is not negotiable."

I began to tell him that he was in no position to make demands, but thought better of it. There was an earnestness about his manner that was compelling. He was not the raving madman of the night before.

"All right," I said. "You can call her."

A broad grin lit up his dark face with rows of ivory and a single gold tooth on the lower right. It was a victory smile mixed with an undertone of gratitude, connecting us for the first time since his arrival.

I asked the orderly to bring his cell phone.

"No," said Youssef, "no cell phone. Mine, at least, has likely been compromised." He pondered a moment, rubbing the stubble on his chin. "Yours, perhaps, or better yet a landline."

The office next door had a phone. I handed him the handset and dialed an outside line. He clutched the handset to his chest, looked up at me, and waited.

"You want privacy," I guessed. "OK. you have five minutes. I'll wait outside."

By the time I reentered the room, the call was over. Youssef looked up at me with a faint smile. His breathing was slow and even. He looked composed for the first time since we'd met.

"Jamilah will be here in twenty minutes," he said. "When she gets here, we'll need some time alone for me to check out the laptop and to bring her up to speed. I need to make sure that she'll be safe after she leaves."

I usually avoided any semblance of joining with a patient's delusion, but by this time I was in his spell. He was no longer agitated and was taking control. His quiet resolve was persuasive.

When Jamilah entered the locked unit for the second time, a leather valise slung over her shoulder, she, too, was calm and purposeful. She was tall, around five nine and now stood fully erect, her bearing almost regal. The curls of her flowing black hair kissed her shoulders, framing an oval face that was almost too small for her body. Her eyes were dark and deep set. Her aquiline nose perfectly bisected her face, stopping just above cupid's bow lips gently kissed with color. I wasn't prepared for such an elegant presence.

I escorted her to the consultation room where Youssef was waiting. He rose to greet her. She placed the valise on the table and they briefly embraced. Then they both looked at me and waited.

"How much time do you need?" I asked.

"Ten or fifteen minutes ought to do it. We'll come out when we're done." He'd by now asserted full control.

Twenty minutes later, the door opened. Jamilah emerged first, no longer in possession of the computer. She walked straight to me, wrapped her arms around me, and touched her lips to my cheek just below my right ear while Youssef watched smiling by the open door.

"Thank you," she whispered at the end of the kiss. "You have no idea how you've helped us." And then she was gone.

Hours later when I reached for the coins in the back pocket of my pants, my fingertips touched a tiny wafer-thin object and a crumpled bit of paper. The wafer turned out to be a Micro SD memory card. On the paper was scrawled a terse message:

"Hide this somewhere very safe and tell nobody. You are part of this now."

2

I MET with Youssef again early that afternoon. I still knew almost nothing of his background and had not yet conducted an intake interview. He sat across from me, slouched a bit, legs slightly apart, and palms up, looking remarkably unguarded for someone so paranoid just hours before.

"What do you want to know?" he asked, again without a trace of the accent from the day before.

"Why don't you start by telling me a little about yourself?"

" I was born in Riyadh, Saudi Arabia. My father was a physician. We emigrated to the United States when I was 11 because my father wanted me to have the educational opportunities that this country offered. It was a struggle at first, because he had to start his training over almost from the beginning, which caused more financial hardship than he'd anticipated.

"I knew some English when I came here. My classmates ridiculed my accent and my broken grammar, but by the end of my first semester, I'd become sufficiently fluent to earn their respect. I graduated from high school in Marblehead third in my class and was admitted to Amherst College, where I graduated magna cum laude in computer science. I got an MBA at Columbia Business School."

His English was now flawless. His Middle Eastern roots lurked beneath the surface and seemed only to poke through under stress.

"While there, I met my wife Jamilah, who was a student at NYU. Jamilah was originally from Lebanon and, like me, came to America as a child, in her case at age twelve. She, too, is fluent in English. We both usually pass for native born Americans, although we still get profiled when traveling by air.

"Go on, Youssef."

"Joe. You can call me Joe. That's what most people call me."

"Joe, then. Thanks for telling me."

"After graduating from Columbia, I got involved with an Internet startup company that went bankrupt after two years. I came away from that venture an expert in web design, which landed me a job in advertising for a cellular phone company. I'm very good at what I do and was earning six figures within a year.

"Most of my work is on my computer. I carry my laptop wherever I go and once even created a major ad campaign while sitting on a beach in Aruba. I was on deadline, but this still didn't go over well with Jamilah, who's usually very tolerant of my working style."

His narrative so far was all fact, no emotion.

"You talked about your father, but you haven't mentioned anything about your mother."

"My mother is dead. She took her own life when I was fifteen." Youssef's dark eyes seemed to scan the horizon and moistened ever so slightly.

9

"That must have been terrible for you."

"By then, tragedy was already too familiar. But yes, it broke my heart again."

"Again?"

"I lost my only brother, my twin, when I was seven. He was my other half, my soulmate. You know how they say twins can sometimes read each other's minds? Ahmed knew my thoughts and I his. We always had each other's backs until...I let him down."

"How?"

"One morning, I woke up and he was gone. Some of his clothes were missing and some money my mother kept in the kitchen. A pair of my shoes was also gone. My parents assumed he'd run away, but there was no note and nothing had happened that would explain why he would leave. I wondered whether he'd taken my shoes as a message to me, but it was a message I was never to decipher. I never saw him again."

"Did you ever find out what happened to him?"

"Never. The police concluded after the first day that he'd been abducted. There was a massive manhunt, but no trace of him ever showed up. After a year of futile searching, he was presumed dead. I knew it was true. The shadows of his thoughts had long since vanished from mine." Youssef shook his head and sighed deeply.

My mind flashed briefly to my own lost twin, shattered and languishing in his hospital bed. I felt a kinship with this man, whose tragedy had unfolded half a world away.

"I lost them both back then," Youssef continued. "My mother was too overwhelmed with grief for the son she lost to take care of the one that still needed her. Suddenly, I had no brother and no mother. My father immersed himself in his medical practice. I was alone and lost myself in my studies. My computer became my best friend."

I saw for a moment the lost little boy before me and had an urge to put my arm around his shoulders and comfort him. I groped for words, but had none sufficient to respond to such unspeakable sadness. I wasn't prepared for what came next.

"She never got over it. She kept all of his things in a room like a museum, along with the news articles about his disappearance and the search. When we came to the United States, she created a similar room in our new home and continued to preserve her memories. She spent hours and hours in that room until the day I found her there hanging, still clutching his robe."

"What an awful thing for a child to see." My response felt totally inadequate to the horror of the moment.

Youssef shrugged. There his narrative ended.

I began to put together the pieces that might explain the psychosis that had brought Youssef to the hospital the previous day: profound loss, years of isolation and lack of nurturing, irrational guilt about his brother's disappearance, and finally the trauma of discovering his mother's body hanging from a noose. And like the seven year old who'd lost his brother, he still clung desperately to his computer. Was that the whole story?

"What's so important about the laptop?" I asked, bringing us back into the present.

Youssef's sad eyes suddenly dilated and he shrank back in terror.

"I've told you too much already. Too dangerous. Too dangerous. No more questions. I must think...must think. No more questions today." The accent of his roots was back.

Bad timing. I'd blown the rapport that I'd worked so hard to build. And I hadn't yet asked about the wafer that Jamilah had slipped into my pocket, presumably as Youssef had instructed. The fingers of my right hand went instinctively to the object, now in my front pocket, that had been entrusted to me. What had I done to earn that trust? And how was I going to recover it?

3

THE FRONT SHEET of my new outpatient was filled out in a tiny manuscript hand, each letter rounded and so perfectly formed that it resembled a computer font.

"Kimi Y Jones," I read, trying to imagine what ethnicity lay behind such a name. I skipped down to her age, 29, and her marital status, separated. Turning to the second page, I found that she had no serious medical illnesses and no previous psychiatric care. She took no medications.

Maria, my receptionist, showed her to my office. I looked up to find a petite Asian woman standing at the threshold. Her slender face was framed in straight black shoulder length hair the texture of fine silk. Her almond eyes were almost as dark as her hair so that the irises and pupils merged to create an illusion of magnitude that seemed to fill the narrow space in which they sat. Her nose was a perfectly formed sliver that divided her face into symmetrical halves. From tiny ears dangled jade drops of teal. Her lips, painted deep red, were as delicate as the rest of her features. Her slender body was wrapped in a silk kimono of flowers on an indigo background. She was breathtaking, a fragile counterpart to the commanding Middle Eastern woman I'd just met in the hospital.

"Please come in," I said, beckoning her to have a seat, but she remained at the threshold, toes aligned with the seam of the carpet. A pair of wrinkles appeared at the bridge of her nose, tiny flaws in a velvet face, the only traces of her consternation.

She looked down at her feet and then at me with pleading eyes, but I had no idea what was wrong or how to make it better.

"Is something the matter?" I asked. She looked again at her feet, lifted her right foot slightly off the floor, then placed it precisely back where it had been. She rocked in place for a moment, stepped away from the doorway, bent down and removed her shoes, depositing them side by side in the hallway to the left of the door. She bowed, crossed the threshold and moved quickly past me to the sofa across the room. She sat in a half-kneeling position with her legs tucked beneath her.

I settled back in my chair, crossing my legs, and began the interview.

"What brings you to see me and how can I be of help?"

"My husband left a couple of months ago," she began in a voice slightly larger than she was, "and I've been having such a hard time. He used to take me wherever I had to go." She fell silent, her eyes moving between my face and my feet. She squirmed and her lower lip trembled. She was staring at the rough black soles of my Timberlands and seemed to be struggling with a decision.

"Excuse me, please," she said at last, "would it be OK if you took off your shoes?"

"Do they make you uncomfortable?"

"Oh, I'm so sorry, Doctor, it's not you or your shoes. It's just that I don't like people to wear shoes inside. It makes me nervous."

I untied the shoes, slipped them off and placed them on the floor by my chair. She looked at me again with a plaintive expression, then down at the shoes.

"What do you want me to do with them?" I asked as she squirmed and clasped her hands together.

"Maybe you could put them outside?" Her question was timid, but I had no doubt that it carried the force of a command. This interview would go nowhere with shoes in the room. I opened the door and placed them beside hers. I had already lost ten minutes of the hour set aside for the history, although the exchange that had just occurred told me volumes about her.

Kimi took a deep breath, letting her hands fall into her lap, and looked relaxed for the first time since we'd met. "O.K. What do you want to know?"

"What's so hard about going out?"

"I just get overwhelmed. There are too many people wherever you go. And places are too big, like the supermarket. The ceilings are so high. I lose my bearings." She shook her head slowly. "I almost didn't make it here today. I wouldn't have if my sister hadn't brought me."

"What happened with your marriage?"

"He said I was crazy." She moved her forefinger in a little ring at her temple. "He couldn't take it anymore. Too many rules."

"What kind of rules?"

"Oh, nothing hard. Just simple stuff, like leaving your shoes at the door. I don't like shoes in my house and I like to keep things clean."

"How clean?"

"I don't like things on the floor. We have hardwood floors and I like to keep them polished. I buff them twice a day."

"What else?"

"I change the linens every day, I don't like dishes in the sink, and I empty the trash when it gets half full."

"Those are a lot of rules," I observed.

"Not so many. If he loved me, he would have stayed."

It was a familiar story. Obsessive-Compulsive Disorder is a harsh jailer that holds captive not only the sufferers of the disease but also everyone close to them. The rules of their households are strict, often absurd, and make normal life impossible. For some people, the goal is to maintain a sterile environment and avoid contamination of any kind. For others, it is to maintain absolute order so that every object and piece of furniture is precisely aligned and in their permanently designated places. For still others, it is to avoid disposing of anything of value resulting in homes overrun with stacks of worthless clutter that would horrify their cleanliness obsessed brethren.

These fearful souls become tyrants, enforcing the rules that they believe keep them and their loved ones safe. Families often put up with the kinds of limits Kimi set on her husband for years, bending and twisting the routines of their daily lives into awkward conformations that barely resemble normal human activities. Indulgence eventually gives way to impatience, then resistance, and finally outrage. Some family members become fed up and escape, leaving their loved one isolated in a lonely prison. Kimi's husband had hung on for three and a half years, still captivated by her exquisite physical beauty and gentle heart until he couldn't take it anymore.

My concession in taking off my shoes provided me a tiny window into what it was like to live in Kimi's world. It wasn't typical of my responses to patient demands and I wondered whether it was meant only to provide comfort to an anxious patient or whether I'd already succumbed to her inflexible realm.

"So are you here for me to help you change the rules?"

"Oh, no!" Her voice now was loud and firm and she shook her head with conviction. "I do love things to be clean. I only want to be able to leave my home by myself. I can't depend on my poor sister forever."

I learned that Kimi's older sister was all she had in the world. She had no children and no other brothers or sisters. Her parents had both been killed six years ago when a bridge they were crossing collapsed and they drowned in their car. It was around that time that her meticulous habits began to appear and she became fearful of the outside world. Her sister had developed a different collection of fears and compulsions, which kept her from setting foot in my office when she delivered Kimi to her weekly sessions. We never met.

Kimi's first session ended much as it had begun. She took my recommendations regarding medication, laboratory studies, and psychotherapy under advisement, but was not ready to commit to any part of it. When she arose from her chair, she turned her back to the door and shuffled backwards in tiny steps until she reached the threshold. She then rocked a bit on the balls of her feet and finally thrust one foot far enough behind her to clear the threshold. When she was finally in the hallway, she put her shoes on in the precise reverse order that she had removed them. She thanked me, bowing slightly, turned, and walked down the hall to the reception desk.

As I sat at my computer to compose my evaluation note on Kimi, I considered the remarkable similarities that had brought two very dissimilar people to my care. Both had lost loved ones to sudden and violent deaths. Both were terrified of the unforeseeable horrors that threatened to shatter their worlds in the blink of an eye.

Youssef's fears had become translated into psychosis: hearing disembodied voices and imagining that enemies lurked everywhere waiting to kill him and his family. His symptoms had led him to flee his home and venture armed into the wilderness for safety, leaving him grimy and disheveled by the time he arrived at the hospital.

Kimi's fears had become transformed into fear of disease and contamination from a world teeming with microbes and led to an elaborate system of rituals that were intended to protect her from harm. She fended off danger with symbolism and magical thinking and arrived at my office door as immaculate as a porcelain doll.

To the outside observer, Youssef's world appeared ever so much more menacing than Kimi's. But both were equally captive to their fears.

4

YOUSSEF SLEPT with his laptop still clutched to his body his second night in the hospital. By the next morning, he was thinking more clearly and realized that he couldn't protect it day and night in the hospital. He held it by his side as he entered the consultation room for our therapy session. He was now clean shaven and had managed to scrub the last remnants of grime from beneath his fingernails. He was dressed in a crisp white shirt and clean Dockers, looking like the computer geek he was and no longer resembling the madman I encountered on his first hospital day.

"Do you have someplace you can lock this up for me?" he asked. "I'd feel better if it were in your personal safekeeping until I leave the hospital."

He was cleaned up and no longer agitated. He was articulate and looked for all the world like a rational man, but his thoughts were still apparently delusional.

"How are the voices?" I asked.

Youssef leaned forward in his chair and I could see the muscles in his temples and jaw tense. He tapped the cover of the laptop sharply with a forefinger. "First this," he demanded, "Will you hide it?"

I took the laptop and put it under the desk. I had a secret compartment in the file room of my outpatient office where I was sure it would be safe.

Youssef settled into his chair. "The voices, Dr. Tripler, are gone. I haven't heard them since my first day here."

"How long had they been going on before you got here?"

"Two or three months at the most, but they weren't there all the time. I could go for days and sometimes weeks at a time without hearing them and then suddenly they would be back for a day or two, then just as mysteriously gone."

"Can you think of anything that might have triggered them?"

"I've thought and thought about it. They never seemed to bother me when I was out of town. I thought there might be some toxin in my home, but my wife hasn't experienced anything odd. My computer work doesn't expose me to any chemicals. I wondered at one point whether the voices were somehow coming from the computer, but that just seemed crazy."

How about your diet? Do you have any odd habits? Any unusual foods?"

Auditory hallucinations typically don't come and go and usually don't resolve without medication. It would be hard to imagine a single dose of olanzapine having such a lasting effect. I went through my differential diagnosis of episodic disorders of thinking: temporal lobe epilepsy, dissociative disorders, pheochromocytoma, and of course drugs and alcohol.

"Nothing. Nothing at all," he said. "I'm practically a vegetarian and eat organic foods whenever possible. I hardly consume any caffeine. My colleagues laugh about the geek who doesn't drink coffee. I have a cup or two of tea a day, mostly herbal."

"How about alcohol?"

"None at all. My religious beliefs prohibit it."

"Drugs?"

"Never! I am the keeper of my body and choose to keep it pure. The drugs you gave me on my first day here felt like a violation," he said, his forefinger wagging at me, "one that I choose not to repeat."

Youssef paused and scanned the room, which was bare except for a desk and the two chairs in which we were sitting. Now his voice dwindled to a whisper. "How private is what I tell you here?"

"Nobody else is listening." I addressed first his obvious concern that the room might be monitored. "I write notes in your chart that the other staff taking care of you can see. I can be as discreet as the situation calls for."

"If I ask you to keep something in strict confidence, can I trust you to do so?" His eyes scanned my face for any evidence of deception.

"As long as you are not at risk of taking your own life or someone else's, I can promise you secrecy."

Youssef smiled for the first time since his wife's visit. This smile, however, was one of irony, not pleasure. "To the contrary," he replied. " It is indeed a matter of life and death, but I am trying to save my life, not sacrifice it. And now my life is in your hands. What I have to tell you now, you must never tell anyone else or I and my family will die."

I felt as though I was about to enter his paranoid world, but considered that what he was about to tell me could provide a clue to understanding his intermittent hallucinations. I sat back, put down my pen and notepad and invited him to begin.

"One day about four months ago, I received an email with the subject line 'Homeland' in Arabic. The body of the email was also in Arabic, in which I am still fluent. It addressed me as Youssef and spoke of sackcloth and ashes and of Allah's vengeance, but made little cohesive sense. It was signed "Your brother, Rafiq." There was an attachment that piqued my curiosity enough to open it after scanning it thoroughly for viruses. It contained what appeared to be a random sequence of several hundred Arabic characters. I had no idea what it meant, but guessed that it might be a coded message.

"I figured that I had received the message in error and forgot about it for the next several weeks until I received another message. This one contained a scramble of Arabic words that made even less sense than the last. I began to wonder whether the attachment from the original message was actually an encryption code with which the subsequent message might be decoded. I retrieved the original sequence, printed out both and held them side by side, but could not make anything of them. I considered calling the FBI, but decided that I was being melodramatic. The messages were probably just pranks.

"Another two weeks passed. Then another message, this time in English: 'Who are you?' I considered whether or not to reply and finally wrote, 'Who are you?'
'Delete the messages at once,' came the next missive.

"'What messages?' I asked.

"'The ones in Arabic,' came the reply.

"'Who are you?' I asked again.

"'Delete the messages if you value your family's safety.'

"'Done.' But I lied. I was now determined to find their meaning.

"'We will be watching and listening,' came the next message. 'If you go to the authorities, your family will die.'"

Youssef began working on algorithms to decipher the codes, but they were beyond his considerable expertise. He never went to the FBI or the police, taking to heart the final threat of his mystery correspondent. Not long after that exchange the voices had begun.

At the beginning the voices commented on his appearance, his behavior, and his surroundings. Sometimes it seemed as if he were hearing his own thoughts aloud. "What a lovely day." or "Isn't that music horrid?"

Later they became more threatening. "Watch your step." "We are watching you all the time." "Prepare to die."

He began to think he was going crazy, but suspected that it all had to do with the mysterious messages on his laptop. He considered destroying it, but something kept stopping him. The message might be critically important. The lives of others might hang in the balance. He couldn't let it go.

When he was sure he was being followed and that his family was in danger, he bought the gun and fled to the woods, computer still in hand. He had no idea where he could hide. By the time the deputies found him after his wife reported him missing, he hadn't slept in almost 48 hours and hadn't eaten in four days. He was deep in the forest more than fifty miles from home with only a laptop computer and a handgun, alone except for the voices in his head.

5

JOE'S TALE of the messages on his computer nagged at me. What if, as he feared, they were deadly serious and lives did hang in the balance? The reference to "Allah's vengeance" perhaps signified a terrorist plot. If I reported it to the authorities based only on a hunch, I would be violating confidentiality and perhaps putting Joe and Jamilah's lives in danger. But if I didn't report it and an attack occurred, I could be responsible for a catastrophe of unimaginable magnitude.

I was eight years old when the World Trade Center was attacked for the first time with a truck bomb, my first vicarious exposure to terrorist attacks. I was sixteen and in high school when 9/11 happened. I remember walking between classes when the news went through the crowd like a magnetic wave traveling the length of the corridor.

"It's a terrorist attack. The World Trade Center's been hit by a plane." Soon we were all glued to TV screens. I can still remember the sick feeling in my gut as I watched the first tower collapse.

"This can't be happening," I thought. "Not in my country. Not here."

I'd watched the images over and over during the next twenty-four hours. The first tower collapsing. Then the second. Each time I watched, I could feel my stomach sink, as if it was tied to these buildings, dragged down by their weight as they fell.

That was also when my path diverged from my twin's. The shock of 9/11 took root in him in a different way.

While I moved forward in my lockstep academic march toward a medical career, he became fascinated with firearms and explosives. A year after we graduated from high school, he enlisted in the Army and trained with the Special Forces as an explosives expert after completing officers' training. Two years later, he was deployed to Afghanistan for the first time. And two years after that, in June 2008, he came home for the last time. At least, what was left of him came home.

Jimmy's right leg had been blown off and amputated just below the hip. The right side of his face had been badly burned and disfigured with scars. But the worst of the damage wasn't visible. The shock of the blast to his brain had disconnected his mind from the world around him. He was unable to speak or move, except for blinking his remaining eye. His ability to respond to others with eye blinks was the only sign that some part of him was still alive inside.

The first time I saw him in his hospital bed, I flinched and looked away. This man, who was once my mirror image, was hopelessly broken. I could easily imagine that I was lying in that bed and he was standing, looking down upon me. Why him and not me?

My brother's fate still reverberated in my thoughts when I met with Joe the next morning.

"Good morning, Doc."

"Good morning, Joe. How did you sleep last night?"

"Like the dead." Youssef flashed a wry grin. His gold tooth sparkled from the reflection of an LED light, seeming to highlight his upbeat mood. "I mean that in a good way." His hands sat loosely across his lap, his feet apart. Sitting back in the upholstered swivel chair, he looked relaxed. No trace remained of the vigilance that marked our earlier encounters.

This was only day 4 of his hospital stay. For a patient who was so floridly psychotic on admission, with both auditory hallucinations and paranoid delusions, the speed of his recovery while virtually unmedicated, was remarkable. Could he have been feigning his improvement to hasten his release? Possible, but the cadence of his voice, his facial expressions, body posture, and grooming were all consistent with the absence of symptoms.

"I think I'm ready to go home now," he said, as if reading my thoughts. "I'm not afraid anymore."

"What about the messages on your laptop, and the threats to your life?"

"Probably just spam. There's enough information online to connect my email address with my Arabic roots. And that attracts all kinds of crazy, culturally targeted stuff. Nonsense strings are typical of spam. I would have realized that if my head was screwed on straight."

He was right, of course. It was all consistent with an elaborate scam. The threats were probably a setup for an eventual demand for money. Just an everyday occurrence in the world of the Internet, magnified through the lens of psychosis.

"So what happens now, Dr. Tripler?"

"I think you should stay another day or two, just to make sure your symptoms don't return."

"Whatever you say, but I'm pretty sure I'm out of the woods. And I do have to get back to work soon. I've missed a lot of work already and can't afford to lose my job."

We agreed that he'd stay another day. If he was still free of symptoms the next morning, he could go. If his symptoms had been triggered by trauma and stress, we still had work to do. There was the unresolved grief over the deaths of his brother and mother. But we would have time enough to address that in my office.

I was looking forward to returning his computer that was locked up in the file room of my office. It gave me an uneasy feeling that I couldn't put my finger on. Completely irrational, but I couldn't shake it. And then there was the memory chip.

The next morning, Youssef was packed and ready to go. Jamilah met us in the consultation room and sat beside him as we went over instructions. He was given no medications. We scheduled his first outpatient appointment in three days. He was to call me immediately if any of his symptoms returned.

The laptop was sitting on the table beside me. I passed it to him.

"What are you going to do with it?" I asked.

"I'm going to wipe it," he said, "and change my email account and all my passwords. Even if it was just spam, I'm afraid the computer and the account have been compromised. Fortunately, my work is all backed up in the cloud. I'll be able to pick up where I left off on a new device."

"And what about the memory chip?" I asked, fingering it in my pocket.

"What memory chip?" he replied, furrowing his brow, looking genuinely perplexed.

Before I could answer, Jamilah flashed me an alarmed look. Her right hand resting on her knee flicked side to side, imploring me to back off. Had it not come from him? I withdrew my hand from my pocket and fumbled for a way out.

"Do you mean the hard drive, Doctor?" said Jamilah, coming to my rescue.

"Yes, that's right," I said, "where the memory is stored."

"I can overwrite that," said Youssef, "so that nobody can recover the data. Nothing at all to worry about, but kind of you to ask."

The creases masking Jamilah's face released and her body relaxed. Her eyes met mine with a look of gratitude and relief. And as they left together, she turned momentarily back toward me with a conspiratorial glance.

What had I done? My only alliance is supposed to be with my patient. And my patient's secrets are my sacred trust. Not the secrets of others. I'd now slipped unwittingly into a conspiracy with my patient's wife, protecting her secret from him, while entering a tacit alliance that felt both troublesome and mysterious. And it made my gut churn and intrigued me, all at the same time.

6

FRIDAY AFTERNOON, five fifteen. I was going through the pile of mail that Maria had flagged to my attention. In the era of electronic communication, paper mail is a distracting annoyance, time lost that I can never reclaim. But aside from the daily deluge of junk, enough of these missives are sufficiently important to screen the lot of them. Legal notices, such as subpoenas, typically still come in the regular mail. So I dutifully ripped open each envelope, setting an occasional one aside and tossing the rest.

At the bottom of this particular pile was an envelope with a single line, written in a forceful, but decidedly feminine script: *Dr. Tripler*. Inside was a handwritten note in the same script:

Meet me tomorrow noon in the courtyard of the ISG Museum.

"ISG Museum?" I knew from my medical school days what she meant. The Isabella Stewart Gardner Museum is located on the Fenway in Boston, a stone's throw from my medical school dorm. Housed in a turn of the century mansion, it contains an impressive collection of priceless masterpieces. While I had only a passing acquaintance with fine art, the museum's courtyard had been a favorite getaway, a quiet sanctuary for reading or contemplation in the midst of the hectic life of a medical student.

I understood the shorthand of the invitation, but how did she know that I'd be able to decode the message?

The next morning, I summoned an Uber and gave the museum's address. I'd decided to accept the invitation only after long deliberation. Who was I going to meet? And what were the risks of such a meeting? If it turned out to be one of my patients, it would be awkward at best and possibly compromising. Encounters with patients outside of the office needed delicate handling. And yet, the terse note was like a trail of breadcrumbs that begged to be followed, a puzzle that needed to be solved.

I arrived at the museum at quarter to twelve, made my way to the courtyard, and sat on a stone bench toward the middle. At exactly noon, I became aware of someone seated beside me, facing the other way, hip to hip. A sweet floral fragrance wafted by me...jasmine, orange blossoms, overtones of fragrant wood. Exotic...and strangely familiar. I flashed back to the kiss on my cheek from Youssef's wife. The same scent. Intoxicating. Trouble.

"Thank you for coming, Dr. Tripler," said the woman beside me. Her accent was precise British English. "Sorry for the cloak and dagger invitation."

I turned to face her. We were almost nose to nose. At these close quarters, her sculpted features were even more striking than I'd recalled. The blood rushed to my face. She smiled at my embarrassment.

"You must be having second thoughts about meeting me here today," she said. "I imagine a secret meeting between a doctor and his patient's wife must cross a lot of lines." Her fingers rested across my hand, lingered for a moment, then drew away. "Don't worry, Doctor. I'm not here to seduce you."

"I really shouldn't be here."

"People break rules all the time," she said. "They do a lot of things they're not supposed to do." She swept her arm across the upper floor of the mansion. "Can you think of a more fitting place for a forbidden meeting?"

She was speaking in cipher, but I understood. The Gardner had been the site of one of the most famous art heists in history, nearly thirty years ago. Thirteen priceless works of art had been stolen in a little over an hour, their empty frames left behind. Rembrandt and Degas, Vermeer, Manet, Flinck. Masterpieces that would never be seen again. A crime that spawned legends, but was never solved.

"How did you know that I'd know where to meet you?" I asked.

"Your ring," she said, touching my hand again. "The Harvard Medical School logo. I figured most students there would know the ISG." She paused before answering the other question in my head. "And most would know the story of the theft. I was drawn to this place myself because of the unsolved cipher that this crime presents. Coded messages intrigue me. And I'm very good at solving them."

She stood and beckoned me to follow as she headed to one of the entrances to the museum from the courtyard. I followed automatically, no longer feeling as if I had a choice about what would happen next. We ascended to the second floor and entered a vast gallery populated by magnificent paintings interspersed with empty frames on the walls and on easels. This was the Dutch Room, that had housed the Rembrandts, Vermeers, and Flincks that had been stolen. The empty frames spoke volumes more than the masterpieces that remained.

I felt my stomach sink and struggled to suppress a shudder, but nothing escaped Jamilah's notice.

"Like the Twin Towers," she said, voicing my thoughts, "when they were no longer there."

A tear rolled down my cheek. She saw it and nodded. Then she moved around the room.

"The thieves have left us a message, if we could only decode it. You see the pattern of the empty frames and of the remaining paintings. The order seems random, but I suspect that it is not, just as the selection of the stolen works was not random." She sighed and raised her arms toward the sky, as if paying homage to the thieves.

"Why did they steal precisely these works, but not the most famous and valuable of the collection? It would have been just as easy to take those. I believe that the thieves were leaving us a coded message, that perhaps the message was the point of the crime. But no one has yet been able to decipher it. Perhaps someday I will."

"Jamilah, why are we here?"

"I wanted you to understand the importance of coded messages, of solving them, not just for their own sake, but to understand the threats that they might pose. I need your help with a very different kind of cipher."

"The one on the Micro SD card that you slipped in my pocket."

"Yes, the cipher on the memory card."

"But Joe said he wrote it off, just an elaborate form of spam."

"Joe doesn't know about the card," Jamilah said. "I made it when I had the laptop. And it's not just spam."

"How could you know?" I asked.

"Because I know ciphers better than Joe does. He has no idea what I'm capable of. I've seen the string and I'm sure it's not random. I just haven't solved it yet."

"Why did you give it to me?"

"When I brought the laptop home, I thought someone might be watching and chose to get rid of the chip for a while. I gambled on your discretion as a doctor. And Joe said he trusted you. I figured you'd keep it safe. Now I need it back, and Joe can't know anything about it or about our meeting. I'm afraid it would drive him crazy again. Where is it now?"

"Hidden in my office. I can get it tonight. I'll be happy to return it to you. Just having it has made my skin crawl."

"And yet, you've kept it and haven't destroyed it," she said, meeting my eyes again. "I've judged you well. Your instincts are sharp. Part of you, at least, knew that the chip's importance wasn't just a figment of Joe's imagination. You knew enough to keep it. And I'm relying on your discretion never to tell anyone about its existence."

She broke her gaze and began to walk away.

"How will I find you later to return the chip?" I asked, reaching out to touch the crook in her elbow.

"Don't worry, Dr. Tripler. I'll find you," she said. And in moments she was gone.

7

THERE WAS A CHILL in the air when I drove up to my office later that evening. I opened the app to disarm the alarm as I approached the door and found that the alarm was already off. Had I forgotten to set it as I pondered my response to the mysterious note the night before? Or had the cleaning crew come and gone that morning without resetting it?

The door was shut tight and locked. The keypad lit up when I touched it and I punched in my code. The lock whirred open. When I opened the door, a cold draft washed over my face from the hallway. I closed the door behind me and moved through the hall until I reached a side office with the door slightly ajar. I pushed it open. Shards of glass covered the carpet under the transom window, glinting in the moonlight. The room was cooler than the rest of the building, the source of the draft I'd felt upon entering. I shuddered, partly from the cold air and partly from the realization that I'd been violated in the place that was most crucially private, the place that housed the most personal secrets of my patients.

I pulled out my phone to call 911, but stopped before touching "Send." Of course the police should be involved. I was the victim of a crime. But once they came, I'd have to tell them about my own activities and whereabouts of the day that I wasn't sure I was ready for anyone else to know.

I moved back into the hall and toward the central part of the building that housed the reception area and the file room. The locked, interior, file room was the most secure place in the building. It had once contained the treatment records for all of my patients. Since the advent of electronic medical records, paper files were being phased out, at least for the medical aspects of the treatment. But I still kept smaller folders of psychotherapy notes that helped me track my patients' narratives from session to session. They were there to jog my memory so I could consider how the pieces of the narratives fit together to explain how my patients' symptoms and behavior had evolved.

In a way, symptoms were my version of the ciphers that so delighted Jamilah. Together with symbols from the patients' dreams and the sequence of their narratives, I found keys to the codes to unlock the messages that they contained, messages that were ultimately intended for the patients themselves. Therapy was a collaboration of exquisite trust and privacy.

It was never my intention for anyone but me to ever see these notes. While they contained the most private thoughts that had been shared with me, they were not essential to the medical record. In an official sense, they didn't exist. And for the sake of my patients' privacy, I felt free to destroy them if necessary.

Discovering the door ajar to this inner sanctum therefore twisted my stomach into a knot. I held my breath as I pushed the door open to discover files scattered on the floor, the exposed notes interspersed with the multi-colored folders. I scanned the shelves, expecting them to be ransacked, but found most of the folders still neatly shelved in alphabetical order. There was a gap between the Q's and the T's, with folders on each side of the gap collapsing into the void.

I got down on my hands and knees to search for one of the "S" files: Youssef Al Saud. When I found it toward the bottom of the pile, I was both surprised and relieved to find it intact, the notes still filed neatly inside.

The sound of a door hinge squeaking and something being dragged across a carpeted floor alerted me that I wasn't alone. I'd assumed the thief was long gone, but suddenly realized that he or she was still there and might very well be armed. Gripped with terror, I sent the 911 message on my phone and looked around for anything I could use as a weapon, but came up empty-handed. I pushed the file room door shut and locked it, then hunkered down until the police arrived.

Within minutes, I heard the sirens approaching, then a loud voice shouting my name and the sound of a dog barking. I unlocked the door and emerged into the reception area, which was now flooded with pulsating red and blue light through the front window. There were four squad cars outside, including a canine unit. A German shepherd sniffed its way around the premises as it strained at its leash.

"Are you all right, Dr. Tripler?" asked one of the cops.

"Yeah, I guess so," I said. "Just a little shook up."

"It was pretty crazy of you to enter the building by yourself," said another officer, a woman who looked to be in her twenties. "The perp was still here. You could have been killed."

"Yeah. I don't know what I was thinking."

We walked around to the office with the broken window. Several boxes of copy paper were now stacked beneath the window. That must have been what I heard being dragged across the floor. Traces of fresh blood were now on the jagged edges of glass in the window. The burglar had made his escape.

"Anything missing, Doc?" asked one of the officers from the door of the file room.

"I don't think so," I said, but I couldn't help feeling that there was something I'd overlooked. I still had to go through the remaining mess on the floor. "What can we do to secure the window?"

"Not much. There's a glass company that offers 24 hour service, but you'll pay a hefty premium and probably still wait hours for them to come. Best we can do is tape some cardboard over the opening to keep out the rain. We'll have a patrol car come by from time to time for the rest of the night. That should at least scare off the scavengers."

I was by now wrung out and desperate for sleep. I made sure to set the alarm as I left the building and headed home, relieved that the expected grilling by the police hadn't occurred.

Halfway home it struck me: the memory chip. I made a sudden U-turn, cutting a rut in the shoulder of the road and sped back to the office. I disarmed the alarm and bolted for the file room. The S's also contained the file for Thomas Seaver. It was within the pages of that file that I'd dropped Jamilah's memory chip. I found the green folder with his name and gathered up the remaining notes inside along with the scattered ones on the floor. I held the notes in one hand and shook them over an empty box. I inverted the empty folder over the box. Nothing fell out. I broke into a sweat as I began shuffling through the remaining files on the floor.

It took more than an hour to methodically reassemble the remaining records, shaking each sheaf of notes over the box as I worked. The floor was nearly bare and no sign of the chip had appeared.

"That must have been what they were after," I thought, "but who could have known that it was there?" Only Jamilah came to mind, but it would have made little sense for her to steal something I'd promised to deliver to her. Perhaps Joe knew about the chip after all. But how would he have known where to look for it?

I turned over the last folder, a red one with the name Ellen Scanlon written on the tab. As I slid it back into its place on the shelf, out of the corner of my eye I saw a dark speck intruding upon the unbroken expanse of beige carpet on the floor.

"A bug," I thought, but it didn't move. I reached for it, my fingernail scooping it up by its edge, then took a deep breath and felt it flow slowly out between my lips. The chip had been there all along. Not the prize, after all, or had it just been missed in haste when I'd interrupted the thief?

A fundamental principle of my medical education was Occam's Razor: Out of all possible solutions to a problem, the one with the fewest independent assumptions is the most likely. I'd been caught up in the midst of a mysterious plot that involved one of my patients and a coded message embedded on a memory chip. And my office had been burglarized, including the file room where the memory chip, and the patient's file, had both been hidden. These events could, of course, be unrelated, mere coincidence. But according to Occam's Razor, it was far more likely that they were connected. One puzzle to be solved instead of two. Perhaps Jamilah, the solver of ciphers, would be able to put the pieces together.

8

THE FIRST NAME on my office schedule on Monday afternoon was Kimi Jones. I smiled. After the turmoil of the previous weekend, the prospect of a session with this delicate, soft-spoken woman was appealing. Treating Obsessive-Compulsive Disorder was challenging, but I felt well-equipped with an arsenal of behavioral techniques. There was an orderliness to the treatment process, a mirror of the orderliness that such patients imposed upon their world.

I found her in the waiting room and accompanied her down the hallway to my office, dutifully removing my shoes before entering. Kimi removed her shoes, hesitated a moment at the threshold, and followed me inside. This time, she carried a shiny blue sack, about the size of a shopping bag, cinched with a cord at the top. She placed it on the lamp table beside the couch.

"If you don't mind, Doctor," she said, still standing, "I'd like to prepare some tea before we talk. It helps me relax when I'm feeling anxious and to concentrate." She pulled open the top of the sack without waiting for my approval and withdrew a small stainless steel kettle, shaped like a pyramid, with a delicate S curved spout, along with a ceramic base with an electrical cord. She placed these on the table and plugged in the base. Then she withdrew a small glass bottle of water and emptied the contents into the kettle.

I watched her methodical performance, more data about the routines that dominated her waking hours, and guessed that this was the beginning of a ritual.

Kimi then kneeled by the table and withdrew the remaining items from the sack: a long-handled bamboo spoon, a small whisk that appeared also made of bamboo, a small, red, round container with a lid, a small porcelain bowl, elaborately painted in a Japanese motif, and two tiny white porcelain cups. I watched as she carefully spooned four small piles of a fine green powder from the container into the bowl.

The sound of the water coming to a rolling boil came from the kettle. Then it shut itself off. Kimi poured a small amount of water over the powder in the bowl and whisked it until it formed a thin paste.

"Matcha," she explained. "It's a highly prized green tea, ground into a fine powder." She beckoned me to join her on the floor and extended the bowl. "Here. Try a sip."

Kneeling, I took the bowl in both hands and raised it to my lips. The fluid was viscous and fragrant, the taste pleasant. I passed it back to her and she brought it to her lips for a delicate sip, then placed it back on the table. The ritual sharing of the bowl presented an intriguing exception to her contamination fears. I began to rise, but she motioned me to stay kneeling.

"Just one more step," she explained as she pushed the switch on the pot and waited for it to return to a boil. She spooned a single spoonful of the green powder into each of the two tiny cups. When the water was boiling, she filled each cup. This time, the result was a thin, pale tea. She extended one cup to me and held the other to her face.

"Drink it, please," she urged. "It's part of the ceremony and it's good for your health. Then we can talk."

45

I drained the cup and felt a warm rush wash over my face. While I might have felt impatient about the delay in our dialogue, the ritual spoke volumes about Kimi.

Ritual is a crucial element of social interaction in most cultures. It tends to be deeply symbolic and evolves to help people weather crucial life passages and to deal with loss and grief. While it embodies many of the characteristics of OCD, ritual, like Kimi's Japanese tea ceremony, is considered a normal aspect of human intercourse. The blurry line between normal social behavior and pathological symptom is movable, but at least partly defined by context. A tea ceremony with a guest in one's house is charming. Insisting on bringing it into one's therapist's office is more curious, if not also a bit charming.

When we were done drinking, she carefully packed up her things and took her place on the sofa, tucking her legs beneath her.

"What would you like to talk about?" she said.

"This is your session," I said. "What do you think is important for me to know?"

She placed a forefinger on her lips and squirmed for a moment, then sighed.

"I told you that my parents drowned when a bridge they were crossing collapsed," she began, "But I haven't told you where they were going." She fidgeted a bit more before continuing. "They were headed to visit my grandparents, my father's parents. Or rather they were going to visit their graves. They were dutiful about going to the cemetery every three months. They felt it was the least they owed them to make up for their suffering."

"Suffering?"

"In the camps. They spent most of World War II in internment camps. My grandmother was there from age eight to twelve and my grandfather from eleven to sixteen. My grandfather dealt with his time in the camps with stoicism. He rarely mentioned anything about it. My grandmother's bitterness, however, seasoned my childhood with the salt of her tears and the sharpness of her rancor. She'd been treated with contempt, as if she were less than human. The injustice to my family always lurked just beneath the surface of my feelings. And I've always struggled with my otherness."

"It sounds like you were very close to your grandmother."

"She was everything to me." She brushed aside a tear with a slender forefinger. "When she died, just a year before my parents' deaths, my world got smaller and lonelier. And I felt so guilty about Andrew. It was a terrible betrayal."

"Andrew?"

"Andrew Jones, my husband. We met as students at Boston University. Marrying a Caucasian was a momentary act of rebellion against the cultural forces that underscored my otherness. I was rebelling against my parents, but it was my grandmother who was most gravely wounded. Her life was steeped in tradition. I don't think she ever forgave me."

I looked at the clock. It was past the hour. We'd used up much of the time with the tea ceremony. And her narrative was so fraught with emotion that I couldn't find an easy stopping point. Interrupting her felt callous.

"I'm sorry," I said. "I know this part of your story is very important to you, but we need to stop for today. We can pick it up again next time."

I stood. She slowly followed suit, picking up the sack and making her way slowly to the door. At the threshold, she did an about face and backed out of the room. Then she was gone.

I'd looked forward to my session with Kimi as a respite from the intensity of the world of Joe and Jamilah Al Saud, an emotional palate cleanser. The tea ceremony promised to fulfill that expectation. But beneath Kimi's gentle countenance was a cauldron of emotions that came to a rolling boil as the session proceeded, bringing my own emotions to another peak.

And my next patient that afternoon was Joe.

9

I FOUND JOE agitated and pacing in the waiting room. He stopped every few paces and cocked his head as if he were listening to something, but he wasn't wearing an earphone.

"You're late," he snapped when he spotted me in the doorway.

"I'm sorry, Joe. My last session ran late."

He cocked his head again, nodded, scowled, then shuffled past me toward my office and sat in a chair in the corner of the room.

"What's going on, Joe?" I asked once he'd settled in place. "Have the voices returned?"

"They're telling me I shouldn't trust her."

"Who shouldn't you trust?"

"Jamilah. They say she can't be trusted." He looked straight into my eyes, his face painted with pain. "I think she's having an affair, Dr. Tripler. She was gone all day Saturday and I couldn't reach her on her cell."

I felt my gut twist into a knot as the blood rushed to my face. I hoped he wouldn't notice my embarrassment in the midst of his own turmoil.

"Have you asked her where she was?"

"Yes, and she said she couldn't tell me. That it had something to do with her work." He tilted his head again and waited.

"Now they're telling me not to trust you, either. I saw her kiss you in the hospital when she came to pick me up. I could see that she liked you. Are you seeing my wife?"

Another gut punch. I'm usually good at handling my patients' delusions. I listen to their conclusions and help them think through the assumptions behind them. But I'm not usually the focus of their delusional beliefs. And there's not usually more than a grain of truth behind them. At least the essence of his suspicion, that I was having a sexual liaison with his wife, was off the mark.

"I can assure you, Joe, that I have no romantic interest in your wife." I felt comfortable that I was within the letter of the truth. This question called for a direct answer and this was the best I could do.

His shoulders relaxed and he settled back in the chair. His lip quivered as if he were trying to suppress a sob, but his head was still. At least for the moment, it seemed that the voices were quiet.

I jumped at the opportunity to change the focus of the conversation.

"It seems like your symptoms have come back, Joe," I said. "Perhaps you should go back to the hospital."

"I can't do that," he said, his eyes glowing with intensity. "I have to be vigilant. I can't give her another chance to betray me."

I considered involuntary hospitalization, but was afraid he would take that as conspiring with the enemy. Besides, he didn't quite meet all the criteria. He'd not voiced any suicidal thoughts or threats against others.

"Then how about some medication," I said, "to quiet the voices."

"The voices don't want to be silenced," he said. "They say they're watching out for me."

"Then what about something to help you feel calmer?"

"No medicine, Doctor Tripler. I need to stay alert. I can't give my enemies an advantage." He got up and began to head for the door.

"Joe, you came here today for my help. You've rejected all my suggestions. How else do you think I can help you?"

"You can be on my side. You can believe me. You can help me discover the truth. Because if I don't, I'm afraid I could wind up dead."

"Dead? How?"

"I told you when we first met that someone was trying to kill me. Remember the messages on my computer?"

"That you decided was spam."

"Now I'm not so sure. There was something about the pattern. I can't put my finger on it. Some kind of code. Definitely not spam. If I could only see it again."

"Will you at least agree to come back to see me tomorrow?"

"What good will that do?"

"So I can help keep you safe, help you try to figure things out, be a witness to what's happening to you."

"Witness." His face lit up just for a moment. "I like that. At least if they kill me, someone will know about it. You'll know what to do. OK. I'll see you tomorrow." Then he was out the door.

I desperately wanted to call Jamilah to warn her about Joe's suspicions, but decided that that would only embellish the deception and add fuel to the fire of Joe's delusion. If she acted in any way in response to my warning, he'd likely infer that we'd talked and become even more mistrustful of both of us. Even a hint of suspicion at the edge of his consciousness might be amplified by the voices in his head. I would have to trust to Jamilah's instincts to pick up on Joe's psychotic thinking and to deal with it as deftly as possible. From my encounter with her at the museum, I could see that she was a keen observer of the behavior of others. Little escaped her notice.

I could only hope that he would be back the next day.

10

"WAKE UP, ZACK." My eyes flicked open. I'd been in a deep sleep. The voice must have been the tail end of a vivid dream. I tapped my phone to see the time: 2:35 AM. I closed my eyes, took some cleansing breaths, and drifted back to sleep.

"I told you to wake up." A woman's voice. Loud, insistent. This time, I got out of bed and turned on the lights. I'd have to awaken fully to purge the thread of this dream from my consciousness. It was still three hours before it was time to get up. I went into the kitchen and poured a cup of milk.

"You know she likes you." The same woman's voice. It had to be coming from my phone. A butt call or a video playing in the background. I looked at the screen. It was dark. I tapped the phone. Nothing was open. I turned it off.

"You think she's hot, too." Someone was playing a horrible prank. I valued my privacy and didn't have any of the listening modules that people put in their homes to interact with their devices. The only other possibility was my computer. I shut it off, too.

"You can't just turn me off. I'm part of you." She laughed. "I'm under your skin...just like she is."

"Shut up!" I screamed. "Get out. Whoever you are." But there was nobody in sight. I went from room to room, turning on all the lights. I was alone.

"He's right, you know. You and Jamilah. In your head, you've already screwed her."

My hands were trembling. Sweat was dripping from my armpits down my sides and from my forehead into my eyes, clouding my vision. My legs began wobbling, which made my whole body shake. I struggled to catch my breath and felt pressure like someone was pressing a blunt object against the center of my chest. I felt like I was dying. No, not dying...a panic attack. I'd never had one, but I'd heard many patients describe the symptoms. That's what it was. The voice was just an embellishment, fashioned by my conscience.

I began to count my breathing to slow it down, then focused on its rhythm. The trembling stilled. The pressure released. My vision cleared. The voice was gone. I finished drinking the milk and went back to bed. The next sound I heard was the rippling alarm sound on my phone, telling me it was time to get up.

I shook off sleep and got ready for the day. The disturbance in the night left me more fatigued than usual, but I was grateful that the voice was gone.

All I could think about during my rounds in the hospital was whether Joe would show up at my office that afternoon. When I got to the office, I checked his appointment time: Two o'clock. I finished seeing my first patient of the afternoon and looked in the waiting room. He wasn't there. I went back to my office and watched the clock, waiting for my receptionist to signal his arrival. By 2:30 I began to despair that he'd ever show up.

"What did you think?" said a voice that seemed to come from across the room. "Why should he trust you?

You want to screw his wife." My breath stopped short. I felt as though I was being strangled.

"Another panic attack," I thought. Then I heard laughter.

"Think what you want," said the voice. "I'm not just part of your panic attack."

My intercom lit up. The receptionist's voice was on the other end.

"Mr. Al Saud called, Dr. Tripler. He couldn't remember the time of his appointment and apologized when I told him he'd already missed it. You had an opening at four o'clock. I told him to come in then. I hope that was OK."

"Yes, thank you. That will be perfect." I started to hang up. "Wait. Is my three o'clock here yet?"

"She just walked in the door."

"Would you ask her if she'd mind rescheduling for tomorrow? I have a terrible headache and need to rest a bit."

When I turned off the intercom, the office was quiet. No voices. I poured a cup of coffee and sipped it as I anticipated Joe's arrival.

At 3:55, I was told that he'd arrived. When I met him in the waiting room, there was none of the frenzy of the day before. He held out his hand and made direct eye contact. I shook his hand, not the usual protocol before a session, and returned his gaze, hoping that my face wouldn't betray the thoughts that had been articulated by the voice in my head.

"How are you, Joe?" I asked. "Are you still hearing the voices?"

"Not so much, Doc. Just a whisper here and there. Easy enough to ignore." He shrugged his shoulders.

"And are you still afraid?"

"Afraid?"

"That someone is trying to kill you."

"Oh, no," he said. "I guess I went a little over the edge for a while. I'm better now."

"And the message?"

"Message?"

"The coded message on your computer. What are your thoughts now?"

"That kind of thing happens all the time. Just spam. Like the Nigerian princes." He laughed. "I'm not worried about that anymore."

Joe's psychosis had come and gone again without treatment. He seemed back to normal, but something was off. The handshake in the waiting room? Something about the way he gestured as he spoke?

"He knows," said the voice. I broke eye contact.

"Something wrong, Doc?" said Joe.

"Just tired," I said. "It's the end of the day."

"I don't need to take any more of your time, then. I'm really fine now."

"Let's make another appointment later this week," I said. "We still haven't figured out what's caused your symptoms or whether they're likely to return."

"That's OK, Doc. I'll call for another appointment if I need you." He stood to leave.

I began to stop him. Given the severity of his psychosis, he certainly needed follow-up.

"Let him go," said the voice. "You don't want to see him again. Not with all your secrets."

"Call if the voices come back," I said as he walked out the door. But I really hoped that I'd never have to see him again. My own sanity was now on the line.

"Imposter," said the woman's voice when I was alone again.

What did she mean? When I first saw patients as a medical student, I felt like a fraud, like a child playing at being a doctor. Imposter Syndrome was a common malady of medical students. Even after I completed training and started my practice, I often felt that someone would eventually find me out. Those doubts eventually faded away as my confidence grew. But now I was beginning to wonder again how competent I was. How could I treat others if I couldn't even control my own thoughts, or worse, if I were crazy?

"Imposter," said the voice again, sounding like an accusation. "Beware of imposters."

11

A WEEK PASSED since my last awkward meeting with Joe. He never called for another appointment. I was both relieved by his silence and anxious about it, wondering when the next shoe would drop. As each day passed without any word about Joe, I began to feel more at ease. And once I'd returned the memory chip to Jamilah, she, too, had vanished from my life. My hallucinations faded away and my sleep had been back to normal for several days.

"There's a woman in the waiting room who insists on seeing you," said my receptionist over the intercom.

"What's her name?"

"She wouldn't say. She just said that you knew her and would want to see her."

I walked out to the waiting room. Jamilah Al Saud stood to greet me, her face quivering. She was biting her lip, holding back whatever emotions were threatening to consume her. The only other time I'd seen her rattled was when I first met her at the hospital right after Joe was admitted. We walked silently together to my office and closed the door.

She looked for a moment like she was going to embrace me, then thought better of it and sat in a chair. When she again made eye contact, her eyes were moist.

"Joe's dead," she said. "They found his body in the river this morning."

My worst fear. I should have insisted he make another appointment or at least referred him to a colleague.

"What happened?" I asked. But I was already certain he'd killed himself.

"He drowned. They haven't completed the autopsy yet, but they think he killed himself."

"When did he die?"

"They said the body was too bloated and decomposed to determine the exact time of death. But the last time I saw him was two days ago in the morning. He seemed fine at the time, so I didn't worry when he didn't come home that night. But when he still hadn't shown up the next morning, I became concerned and reported him missing."

"Do you think he committed suicide?" I asked.

"Perhaps, but you know how insistent he was that someone was trying to kill him."

I wanted to believe that Joe was murdered. At least that way, his death wouldn't be on my hands. To me, murder was tragic, but suicide was unbearable.

"I'm supposed to go to the morgue to identify his body," she continued. "Would you go with me? I don't have anyone else." She looked so vulnerable. It was hard to imagine that this was the same woman I'd once found both intimidating and provocative.

I agreed to go. We drove to the coroner's office in her car. As we entered the morgue, I felt chilled and was overcome with the smell of formaldehyde. I'd seen cadavers during my training as a medical student, but they'd all been strangers. The man under the sheet on the table in front of me had been my patient, whom I'd last seen less than a week before, and the husband of the woman at my side. I felt as though I were in a scene from a movie without any idea of my role.

The diener approached us and motioned for us to approach the table. He held the sheet by the top corners and drew it back to expose the face, which was bloated almost beyond recognition. The mouth was open just enough to see the margins of his teeth, still pristine within the grisly visage. A gold tooth peeked out from the lower right. From the condition of the body, it was hard to imagine that he'd been dead only a day or two. I'd have guessed closer to a week.

I cupped my hand over my mouth and looked away, but Jamilah never broke her gaze. She gestured for the diener to pull the shroud back further. When it was at his waist, she pointed to his right flank, where there was a tattoo of several Arabic characters.

"It's him," she said. "This is my husband."

The diener pulled the sheet back up over the corpse's head, then produced a clipboard that held a two-page form. He wrote Joe's name on a blank line at the top, then passed it to Jamilah.

"Sign here," he said, pointing to one of the lines at the bottom of the second page. "This attests that you've identified the body as your husband, Youssef Al Saud."

Jamilah signed. Then the diener passed the form to me and pointed to the line below her signature.

"You sign here," he said.

"As a witness?" I asked, taking the pen.

"No," he replied, "to attest that you've also identified the body. You did know the deceased?"

"Yes, but…"

"And you agree that it's Youssef Al Saud?"

"I guess so." Jamilah had, in fact, made a positive identification from the tattoo. And the gold tooth clinched it.

"Then sign, please. In these circumstances, it's best to have more than one person identify the body."

I nodded and scribbled my name on the form. The signature was barely legible. The diener then asked me to print my name beneath my signature for the record. As distressed as I was about my patient killing himself, participating in such a visible way in the aftermath of his suicide added to my uneasiness, which wasn't lost on Jamilah.

"Let's go," she said. "We're done here."

As she drove me back to the office, I asked what Joe's tattoo meant.

"It spelled 'Ahmed,'" she said. "His brother's name."

When she pulled up to my office, she stopped the engine and turned to face me before I could get out.

"Thank you for being there, today," she said, touching my hand. "I don't think I could have done it without you." She leaned over and placed her lips on my cheek just below my earlobe. I could feel their soft warmth as she lingered way beyond my comfort level, reminiscent of that first kiss back in the hospital when she'd slipped the memory chip in my pocket. I could almost feel her lips fill out, so slowly did she draw away.

I glanced back at the car as the engine started. Jamilah looked back at me with just a hint of a smile. And I imagined that I saw her wink.

12

JOE'S DEATH shook me to my core. All my doubts came rushing back. I questioned every perception and every decision as I returned to treating my patients who were still alive. My distraction made things worse. I found myself in reveries during sessions, missing words and phrases and asking people to repeat them.

Most people were too wrapped up in their own issues to notice, but a few asked if I was all right and one patient became so irritated by my inattention that he left treatment.

When Kimi Jones came for her next appointment, she felt like an oasis in the midst of the wasteland that had become my world. Her rituals felt grounding and made it easy for me to pay attention to her and to leave my own troubles, like my shoes, outside the door. When she broke out the implements of her tea ceremony, I sat patiently, allowing it to unfold. While I was supposed to be healing her, it felt as though she were ministering to me.

I inhaled deeply as she passed the fragrant bowl of viscous liquid to me, feeling the tension flow out of my body as I breathed out, then took my sip of the thick tea. By the time I'd drained my cup of thin tea, both my mind and body were relaxed and nothing outside the office mattered.

"You were telling me about your husband Andrew," I said once the tea service had been put away.

"My ex-husband," she replied. "There's really not much to tell. We were married nearly two years when I realized marrying him had been a mistake. It wasn't his fault. He was a decent person. We just didn't have anything in common. I think he married me for much the same reason I married him: to shock his family and to assert his independence."

"So you divorced him."

"Soon after my grandmother died. The divorce was amicable and fortunately we didn't have children. My parents were relieved. When they died, I was glad that I'd been able at least to give them that."

"You told me earlier that he'd left you just a few months ago."

"That wasn't quite true, Dr. Tripler. I'm sorry for my white lie. I wasn't ready yet to tell you the real story and admit an embarrassing mistake."

"And you've been single ever since?"

"Yes, on my own." She glanced down just long enough for me to wonder whether she might be leaving something else out.

"There's been no one else?" I prompted.

"Only my sister. We take care of one another. She struggles with her own baggage from our family history. We understand each other's pain and compensate for each other's limitations."

I was grateful that there were no new bombshells this time. We finished the session on time. Kimi backed across the threshold, reclaimed her shoes, and disappeared down the hall.

At the end of the day, I found a small package on top of the pile of mail at my work station in the business office. It was wrapped in a delicate net bag, cinched and tied with a pale green ribbon.

"What's this?" I asked my receptionist.

"It's a gift from one of your patients, Kimi Jones. She said you looked stressed today and she thought it might help."

I untied the ribbon and removed the netting. Inside the box was a small, intricately decorated porcelain vessel containing a fine green powder and a neatly folded paper with instructions in a tiny feminine script for making thin tea. I smiled at the sweetness of her gesture and tucked the box inside my jacket pocket to take home.

That night, as I was dropping off to sleep, the voice came in a whisper: "You're getting too close to your patients, Zack. Watch your boundaries."

It was my conscience speaking. My involvement with Jamilah had crossed some major boundaries, not to mention my fantasies about her. And now I'd accepted a gift from a patient, another taboo for a psychotherapist. No matter that the gift had been left without my knowledge. I could just as easily have returned it to her at her next visit.

"Watch out. She can't be trusted." This time a little louder. I opened my eyes and shook off sleep so the voice would go away. Jamilah was still on my mind. The sensation of her lips against my cheek lingered sweetly and tugged at my guilt. Forbidden and dangerous. What could I be thinking?

I'd been alone for so long. After Jimmy was so hopelessly broken, I never let myself get so attached to anyone else that I couldn't bear to lose them. And my celibacy became a penance for being the survivor. My patients became my surrogates for intimacy, safely contained within the boundary of the doctor patient relationship, a boundary that was beginning to fray.

"Beware of imposters." Now I was fully awake and the voice was loud and clear, but I had no idea what it meant. Was I the imposter, as I'd guessed before, or someone else? Was Jamilah not who she pretended to be?

I got out of bed, found the porcelain container of tea that I'd brought home, and went to the kitchen. As the kettle came to a boil, I looked forward to the relief that the precious brew might bring. I hesitated a moment, knowing that once I'd used the gift it couldn't be returned. I scooped the prescribed amount of powder into the smallest cup I had and filled it with boiling water, watching as the faint green color infused the liquid. When it had cooled a bit, I inhaled the aroma and took my first sip. A single deep breath and I could feel my whole body begin to relax.

The voice was gone. I returned to bed, turned out the light, and drifted peacefully to sleep.

13

I WAS ABOUT to see my first patient of the afternoon when Maria told me that a detective was waiting to see me. Such an intrusion would disrupt my whole afternoon's schedule.

"Ask him if he'd come back at the end of the day."

"She," Maria corrected, "and no. She said the matter was urgent and she insisted on talking with you now."

I left my patient in my office and had the detective meet me in one of the smaller consultation rooms. She was a square-faced woman who appeared around 40, with dark-rimmed glasses and wearing a plainclothes navy suit that was a little too snug around the middle.

"I'm Officer Cramer," she introduced herself. "I'm sorry to bother you, Doctor Tripler, but I have just a few questions about one of your patients."

"I'll tell you what I can," I said, "but what my patients tell me is protected by doctor-patient confidentiality."

"I understand, Doctor," she said, "but this patient is deceased. I'm investigating the death of Youssef Al Saud."

"I thought his death was ruled a suicide."

"I'm afraid some new questions have arisen," said the detective. "I understand you were with his wife when she identified his body at the morgue."

"That's right."

"And you also identified the body. I see you signed the attestation."

"Yes, that's correct." I could feel the perspiration start to bead around my temples. Where was she going with this?

"How certain are you that it was Mr. Al Saud?"

"Pretty certain," I said. "The body was very bloated, but it had a gold tooth in the same place as Youssef did. And his wife identified a tattoo just above his hip."

"Had you seen the tattoo before or were you taking her word for it?"

"I took her at her word. A physician's assistant performed his physical exam when he was admitted to the hospital, so I never saw it, but I had no reason to doubt her. What seems to be the problem?"

"The autopsy was consistent with drowning," said the detective, "but the medical examiner estimated the time of death as at least five to seven days before the body was recovered. His wife claimed to have last seen him less than 48 hours before he was found."

"Which means?"

"Either she was lying about the body being him or she was lying about when she'd last seen him."

"Imposters. Imposters," said a voice from across the room. The detective's eyes went to the beads of sweat now freely rolling down my cheeks.

"Is something wrong, Doctor?" the detective asked.

"She's got you, Zack. Guilty," said the voice in my head.

"No," I said. "Just surprised. I had no reason to doubt her."

"Well, the death has just been ruled suspicious. Probably suicide, but murder hasn't been entirely ruled out. And the wife would be a suspect under the circumstances. Were you aware of any conflict in their relationship?"

"If I were, I couldn't tell you. The duty to maintain confidentiality survives the death of a patient."

"But it doesn't supersede a court order in a criminal action. Be advised, Doctor, that it's in your interest to be candid with me if you have nothing to hide."

The threat behind her words was crystal clear. While she hadn't spelled it out, I'd also come under suspicion. She hadn't read me my rights. She was that skilled at walking the line in her interrogations.

"Guilty, guilty!" screamed the voice from across the room.

"Any further questions?" I asked. "I need to get back to my patients."

"Not for now. But, Doctor, please let us know if she contacts you again. Your cooperation can be crucial to helping us discover the truth." She handed me a business card with her mobile phone number circled in red ink.

"The kiss of death," said the voice once the detective had left the room. "Watch out for the sweet kiss of death. You may be next."

The voice continued to taunt me for the rest of the afternoon. I could barely hear anything my patients were telling me. By mid-afternoon I had no choice but to cancel the rest of the day. I hurried out the door once the waiting room was empty and drove to a bar on the other side of town. But I couldn't outrun the taunting voice.

I seldom drank. Intoxication didn't appeal to me. I always preferred to be in control of my thoughts and my words. But that ship had already sailed. It felt as if an alien intelligence was controlling my thoughts from afar, putting the words in my head and causing them to be spoken aloud.

I asked for a shot of ice cold vodka and tossed it back in a gulp. The cold burn in the back of my throat felt oddly soothing. I chased it with a mug of ale. The fog soon settled over my brain and the terror began to seep away. The voice was still there, but it was muted by the haze over my consciousness and I could no longer make out the words.

I ordered another shot and a beer, throwing caution to the winds. At least I wasn't on call that night. I could afford to get drunk, as long as I was sober by morning.

Through the fog, I heard an indistinct din of voices behind me, mostly male. The bar had filled toward evening and the atmosphere became raucous. Then one of the voices emerged from the din.

"That's him," said a familiar sounding voice close behind me.

"What do you want us to do with him?" said another man.

"Keep an eye on him for now," said the first voice. "There are too many witnesses to do it here."

I turned just in time to see a swarthy man in profile headed for the exit in the dim light of the bar. I did a double take. He was a ringer for Joe.

14

IT WAS IMPOSSIBLE, of course. Joe was dead. I'd seen his body. At least I think it was his body. And yet, not only did I see him in the bar, but I was convinced that he intended to murder me. How ironic that the man who had come into my care because he believed someone was trying to kill him seemed now to be threatening my life.

When I first met him, Joe was hallucinating and was presumably delusional about the threat to his life. Now I was hallucinating and in fear of mine. Was it possible that the man in the bar was also a hallucination and that my fear was the product of a delusion? If I couldn't trust my ears, how could I trust any of my senses? I could only hope that I'd become paranoid, because the other alternative meant that my life was gravely imperiled. And Joe's delusion seemed to be fulfilled by his death. If he did commit suicide, perhaps the peril he perceived in his delusion was based upon the danger he posed to himself. I wondered whether I might also wind up dying by my own hand.

How was I going to get home safely? They could be lying in wait outside the bar. And if they'd been watching me, they'd certainly know where I lived. I was alone, drunk and couldn't have been more vulnerable. And given my earlier encounter with the detective, calling the police was also a dicey proposition. I couldn't tell them that a dead man was threatening my life.

I followed an exit sign to a rear entrance and found myself in an alley littered with trash. It had begun to drizzle. Soon it was pouring. I moved away from the front of the bar, emerging onto a well-lit street teeming with an early evening crowd, and melted into the throng of umbrellas.

"Jamilah," said the voice in my head. I looked at my phone and found Joe's address. That was certainly the last place the killers would expect me to go. If Joe faked his death and was alive, after all, he'd likely be in hiding. He certainly wouldn't show up at home.

I hailed a taxi and gave the driver Joe's address. The taxi came to a stop in front of a brownstone townhouse on a quiet street. In the glow of a lamp, I made out the silhouette of a woman walking into the front room. I rang the bell and held my breath.

The door cracked open. Jamilah peered around the edge, then swung the door wider.

"Doctor Tripler," she said. "Whatever are you doing here? You look a fright. Come in out of the rain."

"I didn't know where else to go. I'm afraid someone's trying to kill me. Not just anyone. Joe. I've seen him and I think he intends to kill me."

Jamilah leaned close to my face and sniffed.

"You've been drinking. A lot, it would seem. You're not making much sense." She led me into the kitchen. I sat at the kitchen table and watched her brew a pot of coffee. She set a large cup of black coffee in front of me and sat opposite me.

I told her about the detective, about the suspicion raised by the discrepancy between the time of Joe's death and her account, about the voices I'd been hearing, and about seeing and hearing Joe in the bar. She took it all in and whistled at the end.

"I must sound pretty crazy," I said.

"You sound a lot like Joe did," she said, shaking her head. "I didn't believe him and he wound up dead."

"So you believe me?"

"I may have to give you the benefit of the doubt. We'll have to find a way for all this to make sense. Another puzzle for us to solve."

"Us," I thought, feeling reassured that we seemed once again to be on the same side. I'd been sure that she'd been lying about Joe and desperately wanted to be able to trust her.

"Jamilah, are you still sure that the body was Joe's?" I asked. It suddenly occurred to me that the tattoo on the body could have been a copy.

"It had to be," she said. "Between the tattoo and the gold tooth, there's little room for doubt. In any case, they will likely have DNA confirmation of the body's identity soon. The bigger mystery is how he could have been dead for so long. I was telling the truth about when I'd last seen him. I can understand why they wouldn't believe me."

If she was lying to me then, she was very good at it. Nothing in her face even hinted at deception. She seemed genuinely baffled by the discrepancy between her own story and the autopsy findings. But nothing in my world was quite as it seemed.

"You're soaking wet," she said at last. "Let's get you dry and warm."

I staggered to my feet. Jamilah caught me by the elbow and slipped an arm around my waist, guiding me into the bedroom. She went into a closet and came out with an armful of Joe's clothes: a pair of silk pajamas, a terry bathrobe, and a pair of slippers. Then she went into the bathroom and began filling the tub.

"If you need help…" she said, locking her eyes with mine.

"I can manage," I said, waving her off, my imagination lingering on the drunken fantasy she'd evoked of her undressing me and gently washing my body in the warm bathtub.

Jamilah left the room. As the door shut behind her, I slipped into the warm water of Joe's tub, imagining myself wearing Joe's clothes, sleeping in his bed, and being cared for by his wife, the intriguing woman just outside the door.

"Imposter," said a voice from a corner of the bathroom. "Beware of imposters."

15

THE NEXT MORNING I awoke with a crashing headache, but the voices in my head were quiet. They seemed to rise and fall at random with no discernible pattern or triggers. Jamilah had washed my clothes and had left them neatly folded on the dresser at the foot of the bed.

I found her in the kitchen, making breakfast. She was wearing an apron as she fried eggs in a pan on the stove, looking as innocent as a housewife in a fifties sitcom. She saw me enter the room and gestured for me to have a seat at the table. She set a mug in front of me and filled it from a pot of coffee.

"How are you feeling, this morning?" she asked.

"I've felt better. I have a terrible hangover. My head is pounding."

"The coffee will help," she said. "And take these." She poured a couple of oval tablets from a bottle of Extra Strength Tylenol, then offered me a small pitcher of cream and a bowl of sugar for the coffee.

The kitchen was modern, but homey and inviting. There was beadboard on the wall behind the sink and a row of canisters against the wall filled with crackers, dried fruit, and other snacks. In one corner of the counter was a cluster of rectangular glass jars, some filled with loose tea and others with tea bags. On a small shelf behind were a half dozen pyramid shaped boxes that held gourmet tea bags, along with a tea ball and other paraphernalia.

"Who's the tea aficionado?" I asked.

"That would be Joe. He had a great fondness for tea, a connoisseur and a purist. He preferred the loose teas. He had a nightly ritual an hour before bedtime to help him relax."

I got up for a closer look at his collection. I opened one of the cardboard pyramids to reveal a silken tea sack, globular in shape rather than flat. In the midst of my brain fog, something about the array on the counter nagged at my attention. I couldn't place it and chalked up my reaction to the combination of my paranoia and a hangover.

I felt better after breakfast, but not well enough to round at the hospital. I left Jamilah's and returned to my home. I found the front door unlocked, which was unlike me. I'd always double-checked at least once to make sure I'd locked the door. There were no signs of forced entry.

I opened the door slowly and entered cautiously, observing the furniture and the position of the rug in the hallway. Nothing was amiss. I spent the next hour going through all my personal things and found nothing missing. The last thing I checked was my hidden lockbox that contained sensitive documents, including a thumb drive with some clinical data from my practice. It was properly fastened and all the contents appeared intact.

By noon, my head felt clear and the voices hadn't returned. I decided that I could handle seeing patients in my office that afternoon. I got to the office just before one o'clock. My receptionist asked how I was feeling. She'd been concerned after my abrupt departure the day before. Then she handed me my afternoon schedule.

I looked over the list. Two patients had been rescheduled from the day before. Third on the schedule was Kimi Jones. I was looking forward to seeing her, hoping that she'd pick up her story where she'd left off last time. I also wanted to discuss the gift she'd left me, a possible clue to her developing transference upon me of feelings that had origins in her earlier relationships. Then toward the bottom was Youssef Al Saud, sending a jolt through me.

"Maria," I said, "Why is Youssef listed on my schedule?"

"Oh, I'm so sorry, Dr. Tripler," she said, seeing my distress. "That appointment was made before he died. Remember, you'd set the time aside in case he changed his mind about coming back. I must have forgotten to take him out of the computer. I'll fix that right away."

"No problem, Maria. It just took me by surprise, given all the odd things that have been happening lately."

I saw my first two patients, which went well. My concentration and perception seemed back to normal. At three o'clock, Kimi hadn't yet shown up. She'd typically arrived early to appointments in true obsessive-compulsive style, so it was surprising that she'd be late. I occupied myself with paperwork to pass the time. The minutes ticked by slowly until four o'clock, when I concluded she was a no show.

After our turbulent last session and Joe's untimely death, Kimi's failure to appear was especially troubling.

79

Maria tried to reach her at her home, but only got voice mail. She tried calling Kimi's sister, but again got voice mail. I felt the anxiety rise in my throat when Maria told me that Kimi couldn't be reached. I began imagining the worst, another suicide or mysterious death. That would be more than I could bear.

By the time the last patient left my office I was beside myself with worry. I got Kimi's cell phone number and tried reaching her myself repeatedly until her voice mail was full. I thought about drinking again to calm my nerves, but remembered the fiasco of the previous night. I considered returning to Jamilah's home, but thought better of it and wound up going home instead.

When I got home, the front door was secure, just as I'd left it. I went inside and bolted the door behind me. After completing another painstaking inspection of the premises, I poured a glass of bourbon, turned on the television in the living room and collapsed in the recliner.

"You're killing them," came a voice from the television. I ignored it...just random dialogue from a TV drama.

"Yes you, Zack," said the voice on the television. "You're killing them."

I turned off the television. The voice quieted. I put down the rest of my drink, which I assumed had triggered the voices, then went to the kitchen to make some tea. The warmth of the cup in my hands felt soothing. My panic subsided as I sipped. My eyes got heavy and I gave in to sleep.

"They're all going to die," said the voice, this time in my dreams. My eyes popped open. I looked at my phone. It was three fifteen in the morning.

"They'll all die sooner or later," said the voice again. This time I was wide awake. "You might as well face it. You're a terrible doctor."

I turned on the lights. The voice stopped talking, but there was no getting back to sleep. I was afraid to turn on the television. There was nothing to do but sit in the kitchen and drink tea until the sun came up.

When it was time to go to the hospital, the voices had been quiet for several hours. I rounded on my patients in the hospital and caught a nap in my office instead of lunch before my afternoon schedule of patients.

"Maybe this one will be next," said the voice in my head as I sat with my first patient of the afternoon.

As the afternoon wore on, the words of my patients intermingled freely with the voices in my head. I struggled to pay attention and conceal from my patients the madness that was bubbling up within me.

"You know you've killed her," said the loudest of the voices toward the end of the day. "Kimi's dead and it's all your fault."

16

I COULD BARELY hear my last patient of the day beneath the din of the voices in my head. They were getting louder and more insistent, dominating my consciousness. As I locked the door to my office and stepped into the street, I realized that it was time to take a break from my practice. It was crazy to try to treat patients when I was myself going mad.

"I should get treatment," I thought.

"You know you can't do that," said one of the voices. "You have too many secrets."

I tried to ignore the voices. They were a figment of my imagination, the reason, after all, that I needed treatment.

"If you tell anyone what you know," said another of the voices, "they'll have to kill you. You must protect the secrets."

As I turned the corner, I saw him out of the corner of my eye. Just a glimpse before he ducked into a doorway.

"No, couldn't be," I thought. "That's impossible."

"Impossible," said the voice in my head. "Joe's dead."

I doubled back and saw a man walking quickly toward the end of the block, then turning the corner. Another glimpse, this time in profile.

I broke into a run and turned the corner just in time to see him disappear around the next bend. Was I pursuing another hallucination? As fast as I could run, he maintained a solid lead. When he disappeared into a "T" kiosk, I followed, bounding down the stairs, and saw him pass through the turnstile headed for the inbound trains. I fished my Charlie Card from my wallet and fed it into the machine. The Braintree train was pulling into the station. He jumped on a forward car and I boarded the second car back.

When the train pulled into Park Street, I watched him leap to the platform and head for the Green Line. Another glimpse of his face in the glare of the subway lights. Joe, or a dead ringer for him. He boarded a crowded train to Lechmere. I entered the same train by another door. I hoped that the crush of people between us would keep him from spotting me. But it might also keep me from seeing where he got off.

At Government Center, a rush of people poured out of the train. As the car emptied, he was no longer visible. I leaped through the door just before it closed and followed the crowd down the platform and up the stairs to the street. When I emerged upon the sidewalk, there he was, just half a block away, breaking into a run.

"He was waiting for you," said a voice in my head. I ignored the warning and took off after him. Riding the trains had given me a second wind.

I followed him as he wound in an out of the Quincy Market, then took off down Market Street past the freeway, winding up at a carousel in a park, populated by local creatures of land and sea instead of horses. He stepped onto the carousel. When it came around again, he was gone.

As I watched the carousel turn, what was happening aboard it transfixed me. As one side passed before me, Kimi Jones sat astride a turtle, a gun held to her temple by a man wearing a lobster hat. As she passed to the far side, there was Jamilah, standing by a hawk, a gun held to her head by a similarly garbed man.

"You must choose," said a voice behind me that sounded like Joe. "Which one lives and which one dies."

My breath stopped short. My throat was suddenly too parched to swallow or to speak. My pulse bounded in my ears, competing with a cacophony of voices from within my head.

"Choose now," demanded the voice from behind me, "or they both die."

Jamilah came around again and met my gaze with pleading eyes as Kimi disappeared behind the central column.

"Save her," said a voice inside my head.

"Her!" I shouted, pointing at Jamilah. "Save her!"

The sound of a gunshot came from the far side of the carousel. Jamilah disappeared around the bend and Kimi came into view, lying motionless and bloody on the carousel platform.

I lunged for her, but powerful arms restrained me from behind, squeezing the breath out of me. When the carousel had made another round, nobody was left on board.

The arms encircling my chest released their grip and pushed me toward the platform. My forehead struck its edge, drawing blood that dripped into my eyes and down my face. I could taste fresh blood on my tongue. By the time I turned around, he was gone.

Kimi was dead. An innocent, delicate flower. How had she gotten swept up in this horrible business? And why was I made to choose? An impossible choice that I'd have to live with for the rest of my life. A barely conscious, spur-of-the-moment choice, driven by the madness of my inner voices. But my choice nonetheless.

And Jamilah? Did she deserve to live any more than Kimi did? Did she even deserve to be saved at all, or was she a part of the terrorist plot that she claimed to be trying to prevent?

The most baffling piece of the puzzle was Joe. He was most certainly dead. I'd identified his body and had seen the coroner's report. And yet, I'd just chased him all the way from Cambridge to the Boston waterfront. I'd seen his face and heard his voice. If one of my patients had told me this story, I'd have considered them delusional, psychotic, hopelessly mad.

I reached for the place that was throbbing on my forehead. It was tender to the touch. The blood was still wet and sticky. I could feel the margins of the gash, which was at least a couple of inches long. That, at least, was real. Whoever had held me back, then thrown me against the edge of the carousel was flesh and blood...no ghost. I heard sirens in the distance as my head started swimming. Must have lost a lot of blood. Voices swirled in the background as my vision dimmed and faded to darkness.

17

I AWOKE to the rhythmic beeping of a heart monitor and felt the cool flow of liquid into the vein in my left forearm from the IV bag that hung from the pole by my head. A nurse stood by the side of my gurney adjusting the flow of the IV while a young woman sat by my head, wielding a needle holder with gloved hands, dipping, twisting, and raising the sutures as she closed the wound on my forehead. A curtain was drawn around me, separating me from neighboring patients. I gathered that I was in the emergency room of a hospital.

A young African American man in a short white coat appeared within the curtain, a stethoscope hanging from his neck. The pockets of the coat were stuffed with instruments. From his uniform and his exhausted appearance, he was either a medical student or an intern.

"Glad to see you're awake, Mr. Tripler," he said. "I'm Dr. Hall. I've been taking care of you. You've taken quite a blow to the head. You've been out for nearly two hours."

They'd identified me from my driver's license, but had apparently overlooked the medical license in my wallet. I hadn't been called Mr. Tripler in a long time. I didn't bother to correct him, welcoming a semblance of anonymity.

"Where am I?"

"MGH."

Familiar territory. I'd done an ER rotation here as a medical student and had done my share of suturing wounds. This was my first visit as a patient.

"How bad is it? Was there a fracture?" I asked.

"We've done a CT. No fracture, and no intracranial bleeding, at least so far. You were very lucky. But we'll need to watch you for a day or two because you were out for so long."

"Can't stay here," said the voice in my head. "They'll figure out you're crazy."

"I really can't stay," I began, before noticing the uniformed officer standing just outside my curtained cubicle. He caught the intern's eye.

"The police have a few questions for you," said Dr. Hall. "He'd like to talk with you now."

The officer stepped inside the curtain and started by apologizing for the intrusion.

"Just a few questions, Mr. Tripler. With injuries of this sort, we need to make sure that they're not the result of a crime."

"Don't tell him anything," said the disembodied voice. "Make him go away."

"It was nothing, officer," I said. "Just me being clumsy. I stumbled and fell against the edge of the carousel."

"Then there was nobody else around at the time? No witnesses?"

"Don't tell him about Joe or Jamilah or Kimi," said the voice.

"Nobody else. I was all alone."

"What were you doing there?" asked the officer.

"Just taking a walk. I was at the Quincy Market and had heard about the carousel. I just went to take a look."

"And you fell and cracked open your head."

"That's right. Just me being clumsy."

"And you're certain there was nobody else around? Nobody on the carousel?"

"I already told you. I was alone."

""Well, there's this one thing," he said, his head tilted, the last word hanging, reminding me of Peter Falk closing in on the murderer in the reruns I'd watched of Columbo. "We found blood on the carousel."

"Of course you did," I said. "I cracked my head open on it." I could hear my pulse pounding in my ears. My head was throbbing.

"Yes, but there was quite a bit of blood...and some of it didn't match yours."

"He's got you," said the voice. "You might as well confess. You told them to kill her. You were complicit. You might as well have pulled the trigger." The pain in my head was increasing. My vision began to blur.

"I didn't see anything," I insisted. "Whatever happened must have occurred while I was unconscious."

"Sorry again to have bothered you, Mr. Tripler," the officer said as he backed out of the cubicle. "We're going to continue to investigate the incident. I'll leave my card in case you remember anything else."

My headache swelled to a crescendo, then slowly subsided. I thought for a moment that I might be bleeding in my head, after all, but decided that it was just anxiety.

The IV fluids had replenished my blood volume. My head was beginning to clear. The medical student had finished repairing the laceration on my forehead. It was time for me to go.

"I really can't stay," I told the intern. "I want to sign myself out." Patients have the right to sign themselves out of the hospital against medical advice, which absolves the hospital and the staff of any liability as long as the patient is believed to be of sound mind. As crazy as I perceived myself to be, I'd not given the staff any evidence of my madness.

He checked with the attending physician in the ER for permission and brought me the paperwork on a clipboard. I scrawled my signature in the requisite places, leaving off the "M.D." that I usually included at the end. The nurse brought a plastic bag with my clothes and removed my IV and the electrodes that were connected to the heart monitor.

I dressed and began to stand, but felt light-headed. I sat on the edge of the bed until the feeling went away. I was steadier when I next stood, but my head was again throbbing. By the time I was outside, it had begun to drizzle. The raindrops felt soothing on my face and the smell of the rain was bracing. I found my way to the T station and boarded the train for Cambridge and the sanctuary of my home.

As the train rumbled through the tunnel, I heard a whispered voice from just over my left shoulder. "They know where you live. You can't hide from them."

I whirled around shouting "Who? Who knows where I live?" But there was nobody there. No one reacted to my outburst. Nobody pays attention anymore to people who talk to the air. I considered the possibilities: the man who looked like Joe who lured me to the carousel, whoever threatened to kill Jamilah and murdered Kimi, whoever might have killed Joe, the police. All threatening in their own way.

When I finally got home, I barricaded myself with the deadlocks on the doors and piled furniture in front of each exterior door for good measure. I stripped off my clothes, which were matted with blood and dirt from where I'd fallen to the ground by the carousel. I started a wash, then ran the shower as hot as I could stand and stood beneath it. The water stung my wound. I raised my hand to the suture line to reassure myself that the stitches were intact. The stinging subsided and the hot water enveloped me. I began to relax.

I wrapped myself in a terry robe and put water on for tea in preparation for sleep. But sleep was not to come easy that night. My head still throbbed from the impact with the carousel. I'd just watched one of my patients get executed and here I was drinking the tea she'd given me.

When I'd drained my cup and headed for the bedroom, I looked down at my hands and imagined them, just for a moment, covered in blood.

"That's right," whispered a voice from behind me. "That's her blood on your hands." I felt a wrenching in my gut and began to retch, then ran for the bathroom and kneeled in front of the toilet as the acid rose from my empty stomach. When the heaving finally stopped, I brushed my teeth to rid my mouth of the sour taste and headed for bed.

Of all the horror of this day, bedtime was the most torturous. Sleep was precious and elusive, slipping away, enticing me to follow a trail of thoughts, tangled among one another in a tormenting mass that filled my head with leadenness.

When I closed my eyes, they wouldn't stay shut. Moonlight filtered into the bedroom around the edges of wooden blinds and reflected from the mirror on the dresser, making the whole room seem to glow. I rolled over and buried my face in the pillow, but couldn't shut out the maddening light.

Sleep came at last, but not to stay. I woke to a jumble of images and glanced at the glowing numbers on the clock that told me that no more than a quarter-hour had passed. And there was the light again, that damned glaring light that seemed to penetrate straight through my skull to my brain and deny it rest.

I lay awake unable for a time either to sleep or to move. My whole body echoed the leadenness inside my head. At last, I managed to drag myself out of bed and found my way to the kitchen. Fumbling in the drawer beneath the sink, I found a roll of heavy duty foil. Making my way to the study, I found a shoebox full of adhesives and extracted a roll of masking tape. Foil and tape in hand, I set to work to create a perfect void, an absence of all light.

Sleep finally overtook me and mercifully stayed until daybreak, when a glimpse of light stole beneath the bathroom door. By the time I opened my eyes, I was already filled with the dread that had followed me home the night before. It sat in my throat and dared me to breathe, but the passage seemed too narrow to allow enough air to support life, only enough to sustain a living death.

When I finally turned on the lamp, I was surrounded by the handiwork of a madman. The window frame in the bedroom was sealed entirely with foil, plastered shiny side out and extending at least a foot over the wall at every edge, my wild-eyed countenance and frazzled hair reflected and distorted in its wavy surface.

I walked into a pitch black hallway and felt my way toward the kitchen. A flip of the switch illuminated rectangles of foil covering every window. The same scene appeared in every room of the house. Only the tiny bathroom window had been missed, permitting a stingy wisp of light to sneak past the light patrol.

I suddenly felt trapped. Even the sparse trickle of air that passed my throat was stifled. I ran for the door, turned the locks, and threw it open, drawing as deep a breath as I could. Standing in the driveway in my underwear, bathed in the dawn light, I was struck by the luminous hues of the sunrise sky that reminded me that the world was still the same…for everyone else. My world was a wicked funhouse of crinkled mirrors, filled with darkness. Whoever now lived in that house was barely known to me, a prince of darkness, a stranger.

18

"**THEY KNOW** where you live," echoed the voice in my head. "You have to get out of here." My forehead ached. I looked in the mirror and saw the neat row of sutures that the medical student had used to close my wound. There was a tinge of redness surrounding the suture line that stood out against my pale skin. I reached up to touch it. No warmth. No sign of infection. The pain was just a normal part of healing.

Where could I go to disappear? My best bet was to head north to either New Hampshire or Maine, both familiar territory from my youth. I checked out the weather on my phone. The temperatures up north were beginning to drop, sixties in the daytime, forties at night. The foliage was starting and would soon be spectacular. I decided to head for the coast of Maine and packed my suitcase with warm clothing. The thought of spending time in a place that I loved lifted some of the weight from my heart.

I was on the road by mid-morning, winding my way through the streets of Cambridge toward I-95 with no idea of my destination. I'd just play it by ear until I was far enough away from home to elude pursuit. I scanned my surroundings and found no evidence of anyone following me. Once on the highway, I pressed the accelerator until I was going seventy-five, then set the cruise control. As desperately as I wanted to flee, I was careful to keep my speed below the limits that would attract the highway patrol. A speeding ticket could blow my cover. I'd set up a virtual private network on my phone and disabled tracking to make it harder for anyone to find me.

A little more than an hour and I passed the exit for Kittery, the southernmost coastal town in Maine, then a short while later the exit for Ogunquit. Both were popular weekend getaways for Bostonians and were usually flooded with tourists well into the fall. Both too close and too populous.

"Keep going," said the voice in my head. "Still not far enough."

At the two-hour mark, I took the exit for Portland. I was starting to get hungry, the gnawing in my stomach beginning to eclipse the pain in my forehead, but still dared not stop. I followed the signs to US 1, the coastal road, and continued to head north. Another hour and a half and there were signs for Camden. As I rolled over the last rise into view of the town, my hunger was peaking and I desperately needed to pee. It was well past tourist season this far north. There was a decent scattering of empty parking places along the sidewalks. I pulled over, stepped out of the car, and scanned my surroundings. Nobody seemed to be watching. I took a deep breath of the crisp fall air and let it flow out slowly between my lips. For the first time since I awoke that morning, my heart wasn't racing. Peace was beginning to descend upon me. Even the voices were quiet, at least for the moment.

I walked the street, passing restaurants and gift shops and wound up at the Camden Deli, a coffee shop and bakery that was open for lunch. The menu offered a generous selection of sandwiches. I eyed the lobster roll, but settled on a Reuben and coffee and found my way, by way of the restroom, to the upper deck overlooking the harbor. I felt my pulse rate drop another notch as I watched a schooner glide lazily from its place along the dock through the harbor toward the open sea. It was hard to imagine that less than twenty-four hours earlier, I'd witnessed the murder of one of my patients and had seen what appeared to be the ghost of another.

This seemed like as good a place as any to spend the next few days. My next dilemma came into focus as I paid for my lunch. I automatically pulled out a credit card, then thought better of it and paid in cash. Using my credit card would be another way to track me. I had a little more than $600 in my wallet, which wouldn't buy me more than a night or two in this tony village, even off-season. Getting cash at an ATM would also be risky. Sleeping in my car wasn't much of an option with the night-time drop in temperature. And traveling further north would require filling the gas tank, another expense I could ill afford.

What could I sell or pawn? My most valuable possession was my cell phone, with which I wasn't prepared to part. Work was another option, but it would have to be for someone who would pay in cash and not require identification. That left out most of the service jobs in town.

I got back in my car and started driving west, away from the harbor and the center of town. The road wound around the circuitous contour of a lake, then up and down hills into the countryside, surrounded by farms. I passed a hand-lettered sign that said "farm hand wanted" and turned sharply down the dirt driveway. A few hundred feet and the farmhouse came into view. I pulled up in front of the house, got out of the car, and mounted three wooden steps to the front porch. A rickety screen door hung slightly ajar. I swung it open and knocked.

The hinges on the front door creaked as it opened to reveal a stocky, balding, middle-aged man with a russet beard, dressed in overalls and a green plaid shirt. He looked me up and down, his eyes lighting momentarily on the stitches in my forehead, then glanced at my almost new SUV. I suddenly felt self-conscious about my pressed, white button-down shirt, dress jeans, and upscale Nikes, hardly the outfit of someone looking for work as a farm hand.

"Ayuh?" he said, after taking it all in.

"I saw your sign," I said. "I could use some work."

"Let me see your hands," he said. I held out my hands, palms up. He shook his head slowly.

"Why on earth would you want to work in the dirt? You look like you've never done an honest day's work in your life."

"I've been driving all day and lost my credit card. I may have left it at a restaurant hours back down the road. I need money for gas and a place to stay. I'm willing to work for both." My story was full of holes. Even a farmer in rural Maine would know that in the age of cell phones there were lots of ways to get money and to pay for things.

He stared at me for what seemed like an hour, shook his head again, then turned and disappeared down a hallway. When he came back, he had an armful of clothing: overalls and a plaid shirt much like his. He tossed the pile at me. I caught it clumsily.

"These should fit," he said. "They belong to my son. I can't do anything about your shoes, though. They're probably going to be toast by the time you're done. I don't know what you're running from, son, but I guess it's none of my business. There's a room in the back where you can stay. I'll pay you five dollahs an hour cash plus room and board."

I changed my clothes. The loose overalls felt surprisingly free and good. When I came back out, he beckoned me to follow him out to the field behind the house. There were expanses of long green hay as far as the eye could see, broken in the middle with flattened spans topped with long shallow piles of flaxen hay that had dried in the sun. Off to one side was an odd cylindrical contraption about as tall as I was, attached to a tractor. It was hinged in the middle at the top and listed to one side.

"That's my baler," said the farmer. "It has a broken axle and it'll be days before it's fixed. We'll have to bale the hay by hand." He walked around the tractor and the baler toward what looked like a large crate standing on end, a pump handle hanging off the top. He swung one of the vertical panels open by a hinge, revealing a horizontal flat piece of wood that fit neatly within the crate, hanging down within it by a 2X2 pole. He grabbed the pump handle with one hand and lifted. The flat piece inside the crate plunged close to the ground. He pulled the handle down until the flat piece cleared the top. Then he closed the hinged panel.

"I'll show you what to do." He walked a few steps down one of the cut rows, reached down and retrieved a pitchfork that had been half buried in one of the piles of hay. He held it parallel to the ground at the start of a pile and pushed through the pile. The hay accumulated around the tines of the pitchfork into a ball. He lifted it and swung the hay into the top of the crate, then lifted the handle to plunge the compressor on top of it.

"You keep at it until the baler is full. Then open the door and dump it out." He plunged the tines into the ground uncomfortably close to my feet. "Come find me when you've done twenty bales."

I pulled out the pitchfork and got to work. He'd made it look easy, but it took a while to get the angle of the fork just right to pile up the hay without getting the tines stuck in the ground. Fifteen minutes and I had the rhythm. A half hour and I'd made my first bale, an almost perfect rectangle as it tumbled from its enclosure. It was a surprisingly satisfying accomplishment. But the thought of repeating this feat another nineteen times was daunting.

I got better as the afternoon wore on and completed the last bale by the time the sun had dipped below the tree line. I returned to the house and knocked on the door. The farmer stepped outside and looked over the neat rows of nearly identical bales. A smile crept over his face.

"Not bad for a city boy," he said. "Let's get some suppah." His last syllable seemed to hang on the air.

Inside the kitchen was a plank style wooden table filled with platters of vegetables. A loaf of crusty bread and a long bread knife sat on a board along with a colander of spaghetti and a bowl of sauce. He brought a jug of cider from the fridge.

"My wife's at her sistah's for the week. I try to keep it simple when I'm on my own."

We ate most of our meal in silence. I was famished from the labor. Food never tasted so good. When we were done eating, he walked with me to my room and showed me where to find blankets and towels. There was a simple shower stall, but the water was hot and the pressure adequate.

As I let the water pour down on my sore muscles, I realized that I hadn't heard any voices the whole time I was working. The work had been a welcome distraction. Perhaps I was getting better. I pulled on my flannel pants and hoodie and slipped, exhausted, into bed.

"You can run, but you can't hide," said the voice as I passed through the twilight stage of sleep. "I'm not done with you yet."

19

I AWOKE to the early morning light filtering through the sheer curtains over my bedroom window. As I lay motionless in bed with eyes open, I listened for the voices. All I could hear was the sound of birds through the open window. So far so good.

A fresh set of work clothes was piled on the dresser by the foot of the bed, left there by my host as I slept. I got dressed and headed for the kitchen, where I found him at the stove making pancakes in a cast iron skillet. A large jug of maple syrup sat on the table alongside a bowl with a mound of butter. A pot of coffee was warming over a low flame on another burner on the stove.

"Mornin', City Boy," he said. "Sleep well?"

"Like the dead," I said. "You can call me Zack. Sorry I didn't introduce myself yesterday."

"Figured it was none of my business. You'd tell me when you were good and ready. I'm Otis." He slid a large plate in front of me and piled it high with pancakes from the skillet.

"Thanks, Otis. What's on my schedule for today? More baling?"

"Time enough for that. Thought I'd give you a break this morning. Getting ready to paint the barn, but first it needs scraping and washing."

"Pressure washer?"

"Not how we do it around here. You'll scrape it with a blade, then scrub it by hand to get as much of the old paint off as possible. There's an extension ladder on the ground around the side of the barn. But first eat your breakfast. You're gonna need it."

I've always had a fear of heights, especially ladders, but I didn't want to admit this to Otis. So I screwed up my courage as I headed for the barn. The ladder was huge and heavy. I managed to prop it against the side of the barn close to the peak. I tucked the putty knife in a pocket of my overalls, filled a bucket with sudsy water and a bristle brush, and gingerly climbed the ladder. I found it solid and stable and grew bolder as I climbed. I didn't look down.

"Exposure therapy," I thought. "This will get easier." In my practice, I'd helped patients overcome fears by exposing them to the things they'd been avoiding. One way was to start gradually with something a little scary and build toward the most terrifying instances. For example, first looking at pictures of spiders and winding up letting spiders crawl all over their hands. The other way, called "flooding," involved starting with the worst case scenario, while preventing escape until it was no longer frightening. Flooding it was. If I were to stay on the farm, I had no choice.

By mid-morning, I'd washed the uppermost section of siding and was working my way down the ladder. The anxiety had long since drained away. I was scraping and scrubbing as if I was planted firmly on the ground. Like the hay baling, I discovered a rhythm to the work that felt almost meditative and a second wind that seemed endless. Breathing in the crisp, fall air and the scent of the surrounding balsam, I felt at peace. All I could hear were the birds, the occasional sounds of squirrels skittering over fallen leaves, and the distant mooing of cows. No voices. All was quiet inside my head.

By noon on the fourth day, I'd finished scraping the barn and was ready to start painting. I decided to work top down, as I had with the scraping, and made my way after lunch to the top of the ladder. About an hour into the work, the quiet around me was interrupted by the sound of an engine overhead and the rhythmic whirring of helicopter blades. The chopper was circling just overhead, low enough for me to feel its wash as it crossed over the barn. Between the wind from the turning blades and the unsettling awareness that I might be the object of the aerial surveillance, I nearly lost my balance. My awareness of height was suddenly all too palpable. After a few minutes, the chopper rose and veered away. I watched until it disappeared from view, grateful that we'd moved the SUV into the barn soon after I'd arrived.

As I approached Otis's house for supper, a police car stood in front of the stoop. I fell back and watched from a distance as the officer mounted the steps and Otis emerged to greet him. The conversation appeared animated, punctuated by gestures. The officer pointed toward the barn. Otis shook his head from side to side and raised both hands in a gesture of ignorance. Once the car pulled away, I waited twenty minutes before heading to supper.

"What was that all about?" I asked Otis as he spooned mashed potatoes onto my plate.

"The police car? They're looking for a stranger from out of town. Said he was a doctor. Been missing nearly a week."

"What did you tell him?"

"That I haven't seen any strangers around here. That I know my farm hands and vouch for them."

"Thanks, Otis. You didn't have to cover for me."

"Like I said, whatevah you're running from is none of my business. Besides, this is a small town and I know every officer on the force. This fellah was the real stranger."

Bad enough that the police might have been looking for me. Even worse if it was someone else.

On my sixth day on the farm, I finished painting the barn. I stood back and admired my work, which was satisfying in a concrete way that the more subjective results of my usual work could never be. In the field beyond were sixty bales of hay that were also my handiwork. My muscles ached from the work, but my body felt strong and healthy. I'd slept better than I'd slept in years. And the voices never returned.

Part of me wished that I could stay on the farm forever, but I had a life and responsibilities to get back to and it was past time to get the stitches out of the wound on my forehead. My paranoia had subsided along with the fading of the voices. I wondered whether the fear that had driven me from my home had just been my imagination working overtime. I even began to doubt whether what I'd witnessed on the carousel was real despite the blood that had been found on the carousel where I'd watched Kimi get murdered.

It was time, though, to confront my fear. The lesson of the ladder wasn't lost on me. The best way to overcome fear was to deal with it head on. If I could feel comfortable near the top of a sixteen-foot extension ladder, I should certainly be able to feel safe in my own home.

And then there was Jamilah. Had she survived the events at the carousel and had she ever returned home? I was burning to find out. And the thought of seeing her again excited me in a way that I was reluctant to acknowledge.

"Nice job," said Otis from over my shoulder. "That barn nevah looked so pretty."

"Thanks, Otis," I said. "I'm glad I got to finish the job. It's time for me to go home. I've been away too long."

"Sorry to see you go. I don't know what you've been running from, but I hope it all works out. Anyone willing to work as hard as you have must be a good man. I'll miss having you around."

Before I left the next morning, Otis handed me a roll of bills: $240 in twenties, my pay for nearly a week's work. So little money has never felt so satisfying. It would be more than enough to keep me off the grid until I got back to Cambridge.

I wended my way down coastal US 1, enjoying a last Maine lunch at a roadside Lobster Pound before joining I-95 at Ogunquit for the rest of the journey. I was careful to stay well below the speed limit in order to avoid attention. My pulse quickened at every sighting of a State Police cruiser in my rearview mirror, but they all passed me uneventfully. By mid-afternoon, I was passing through Somerville and soon pulled into my driveway.

A pile of mail lay at the front door. Stopping the mail would have been the last thing on my mind when I'd fled. When I went inside, the aluminum foil still covered most of the windows. I stripped it off and threw open most of the windows to air out the house. It felt good to be home.

I opened my computer and checked my email for the first time in nearly a week. There were over a hundred messages, including many from colleagues and friends who were covering my practice during my recovery from the head injury. Several expressed concern about the foil that was visible in the windows from outside my home. The messages became increasingly frantic as they went unanswered. The most recent messages indicated that they were about to report me missing. I wrote back and apologized for my failure to respond, indicating that I'd decided on the spur of the moment to spend a week in Maine to help me recover. It had been very helpful, and I would soon be ready to return to work and resume responsibility for my practice.

Then I turned my attention to Jamilah. Her home was just under two miles from mine. I decided to walk there with no plan for what I'd do when I got there. I stopped across the street and surveyed the home. Dusk was falling, but no lights were visible inside. Her home had a garage, so I had no way to know whether or not her car was there. In the time we'd known one another, she'd communicated with me through my office and by handwritten notes. We'd never exchanged cell phone contacts or email addresses, respecting the discretion that our peculiar relationship deserved, discretion that I'd blown with my impromptu nocturnal visit.

I thought about knocking on the door, but remembered my encounter with the spectral figure that looked like Joe. I didn't want to risk the possibility that at this point he could be the one to answer the door. Instead, I walked to a nearby tavern for some supper. I resisted the temptation to accompany my Reuben with a beer. My head needed to stay clear.

It was dark by the time I left the restaurant. When I walked past Jamilah's home again, it was still dark. My heart sank. I appreciated what my friends must have felt when they went looking for me and thought I'd disappeared. I was beginning to think that I'd never see her again, which also meant that whatever she might know about the mysteries that surrounded me would be lost to me forever.

20

THE VOICES had been gone for nearly a week. I was still grieving the deaths of two of my patients, struggling with the guilt I felt for my part in each of these deaths. It isn't unusual for psychiatrists to lose patients to suicide, but second thoughts and self-recriminations are an inevitable consequence. Unlike surgical patients or oncology patients, our patients aren't ever supposed to die. Suicide implies a grievous error, something overlooked, a treatment gone horribly wrong.

My role in Kimi's death was something else altogether. I was a bystander, a witness. But I'd been forced to make an impossible choice that left me complicit in her murder, a murder that hadn't yet been discovered. She'd been reported missing. Her sister had called my office to apologize for her missing an appointment. She'd simply disappeared. A search was launched, but as the days passed it became less and less likely that she'd be found alive. For me that was a certainty. I'd watched her die. I was the only person, other than the killers, who knew exactly what had happened to her.

So why didn't I report it to the police? Was I more afraid that they'd find me complicit in her murder or that they'd take my wild story as a sign that I was hopelessly mad and lock me up forever? I'd claimed to have wound up at the carousel by chance and to have split my head on its edge out of clumsiness. I'd attributed other gaps in my personal narrative to my concussion.

Jamilah seemed also to have disappeared, but I had no idea if there was anyone else left in her life beside me who would miss her and report her missing. And to the outside world, I left her role in the events at the carousel shrouded in my presumed amnesia.

All I wanted to do now was to reclaim some semblance of normalcy in my life. It was too soon to be back to work. My doctors insisted on at least a month's recovery from the head injury before considering seeing patients again. When I'd awakened in the hospital emergency room, I was still actively hallucinating, but the attending doctor attributed that to the concussion. I didn't correct their impression.

As I walked by the river watching the racing shells glide silently through the water in the early morning light, I reflected on more innocent times when I was responsible only for myself and my studies and I dreamed of leading a worthwhile life helping others. How had I wound up with so much innocent blood on my hands?

I suddenly felt a chill in the morning air make the hairs stand up on my arms. Someone was watching me. I was sure of it. I quickened my pace and heard footsteps behind me falling on the dirt path and keeping pace with me. I broke into a run. The slapping of shoes against the ground behind me grew faster and louder as my pursuer gained on me. My breathing became labored. I couldn't keep up the pace.

I felt warm breath on the back of my neck as one arm encircled my waist and another held a wad of cloth over my mouth with a pungent, alcohol-like smell. I looked down at the hand on my waist, which was tawny and slender. A woman's voice whispered in my ear. Her breath against my cheek felt soft and soothing.

"Breathe deeply, Doctor," said the voice. "It's time to go to sleep."

*****

The next thing I knew I was lying in a hospital bed unable to move or speak. My lungs were supplied with air that came in pulses from a machine that was connected by a tube to the tracheostomy in my neck. Jimmy stood by my bedside, his lips closed in a tight line, his head shaking from side to side. His eyes squinted as if he were trying to look at me and not see me all at the same time.

The door opened. Jamilah entered the room and took her place by Jimmy's side. She placed a hand on his cheek and whispered something in his ear. He nodded.

"I'm sorry, Zack," he said, turning back toward me. "I just couldn't stand to lie there any longer. I had to switch places. It was your turn."

I struggled to reply, but all I could do was blink.

"See, Jamilah," he said, "He can hear us."

Jamilah sat on the side of my bed, placed her palm over my hand and leaned in close enough for me to smell the fragrance of her skin and feel her breath on my face.

"Beware of imposters," she whispered in my ear, her breath suffusing my ear canal with warmth. "Nothing is as it appears."

Then I was standing by the bedside and Jimmy was in his usual place in the bed, Jamilah standing beside him, looking right at me. She leaned over and kissed him first on his cheek and then on the mouth, a lingering kiss. As she arose, his eyes opened wide, he took a deep breath, reached for the breathing tube to disconnect it from the tracheostomy, and sat bolt upright. I rushed to embrace him, but he dissolved before my eyes.

*****

When I awoke from my fever dream, everything was out of focus. I was looking down a long corridor, a woman's slender silhouette backlit and framed in the opening at the far end before vanishing around the corner. My wrists were bound behind me.

"Jamilah," I tried to shout, but my voice was raspy and weak. What difference would it have made, anyway, whether she'd heard me or not. It appeared that she was the enemy, after all. I'd been a fool to trust her. Even in my dreams, she was a cipher who spoke in riddles and wielded power over life and death with her kiss.

Then a man rounded the corner and appeared silhouetted in the door at the end of the corridor before approaching. His face was in the shadows until he was ten or fifteen feet away, when his features gradually emerged from the darkness like a ghost coming to life. By the time I could make out his face, I gasped. It was Joe.

21

IF WE PAY attention to our dreams, they can tell us things that might otherwise remain hidden forever. Many of their lessons are about the dark fantasies and guilty wishes that we keep secret even from ourselves, thoughts that would be too painful to acknowledge because they violate the most fundamental principles we hold dear. These deeply repressed fantasies are disguised and transformed, becoming allegories for what lies beneath. In place of the linear logic of our conscious thoughts appears the poetic symbolism of the unconscious part of our mind.

Dreams can also provide keys to unlock mysteries in the external world. Remnants of our experience of the previous days or weeks become grist for the mill that creates our dreams. If we're willing to listen, the puzzle pieces they contain can fall neatly into place. So it was with the drug induced dream from which I'd just awakened.

I looked into the eyes of the man who stood before me, the man I recognized as Joe, and flashed back to the content of the dream. I'd switched places with my identical twin, a man who had all but died and was resurrected in the exchange. And then followed the admonition: "Beware of imposters."

"Ahmed," I said. "You're Joe's brother."

"Very astute, Doctor," replied Ahmed, breaking into a smile that revealed a gold tooth like Joe's, but on the wrong side of his mouth. "But now I'm known as Hamzah."

"Then Joe is really dead," I said.

"Sadly so," replied Hamzah, the smile vanishing from his face. "I regret that I will never get to know him. We were once inseparable. I wish it could have gone another way."

"Did you kill him?"

"The mission demanded it. It was the only way I could replace him. It was my destiny."

"What could possibly justify murdering your brother...your twin?"

"My brothers are legion. My duty to them and to our cause overrides any single relationship in my life, even if it is by blood."

As I listened to his confession, I realized that it meant that I was intended never to leave this place alive. A man with little compunction about murdering his twin would certainly not leave witnesses behind. My only shred of hope hung on the possibility that Jamilah might show me mercy. I flashed back to her role in my dream in search of any clue to how I might appeal to her for my life.

"Jamilah," I said, "Was she part of this from the beginning? Did she conspire with you to kill her husband?"

"Jamilah?" He seemed to turn my question over in his mind. His smile this time was slow, cryptic. "What makes you think she's a part of this?"

"I saw her leaving this hallway just before you appeared."

"Ah, yes," he said, the smile widening slightly. "Jamilah knew. She's the one who gave the order."

"Can I see her?"

"I'm very sorry. That won't be possible. But I'm afraid it wouldn't help your situation, anyway."

Hamzah moved behind me and released my bonds. "These won't be necessary," he said. "There's no way out of here. You will be our guest for a while before you play your destined role in our plan. You might as well be comfortable."

"It was you who led me to the carousel. Why? And why would you murder my patient?"

"You were sadly too much of a loose end and we couldn't just kill you without attracting attention. You'd have eventually figured out that I'd taken Youssef's place. If you believed you'd gone mad and were complicit in a murder, we figured you'd keep your story to yourself. And if you told it, it would sound so crazy that nobody would ever believe you. Soon the loose end will be tied for good."

Hamzah led me into a room that contained a circle of brightly colored satin covered cushions around a low table. Upon the table was a teapot, four small cups, and a porcelain vessel with a small wooden spoon. Hamzah took his place on one of the cushions and beckoned for me to sit. He removed the top of the teapot, withdrew a porous steel ball on a chain and filled it from the vessel with the wooden spoon. He returned the tea ball to the pot and filled the pot with water from a steaming electric kettle.

"It needs time to steep," he said. "I share my brother's love for tea. There is no greater pleasure. I hope you will join me." His manner was polite, matter-of-fact, as if we had just met in a cafe or he'd invited me into his home, not the manner of a man who intended to end my life.

This odd scene brought to mind the equally odd memory of Kimi Jones's tea ceremony in my office. Both experiences were out of the context of the encounters. One was between a doctor and his patient, the other between a murderer and his intended victim. All I could do was accept the cup that was handed to me. I brought it to my face and instinctively inhaled. It was fragrant and surprisingly pleasant.

Hamzah took a sip from his cup and gestured for me to drink. I took my first sip. As I sipped my tea, he began to speak.

"You must know part of my story," he said. "Youssef would have told you about me and about my disappearance when I was seven. He had no idea that I'd survived."

My curiosity was aroused. I wanted to know how Joe's brother had been turned into a ruthless zealot. His story was at least a distraction from pondering my fate. I sipped and listened, slipping into my role as therapist and losing myself in his narrative. Perhaps I would learn something that might help me change his mind about killing me.

"I was abducted in the middle of the night from the room I shared with my brother. As I was swept away, I grabbed Youssef's shoes. It was a moment of instinct to take something of his, something intimate that smelled of him so that we could stay connected. And it worked for a while. It helped me remember. But it wasn't enough."

I smiled, remembering Joe's story of the missing shoes and appreciating the closure that Hamzah's story brought to that mystery.

"I was sold to a nomadic tribe and raised by my adoptive parents to be a warrior. They were members of a jihadist organization that was affiliated with Al Qaida. As a teenager, I was indoctrinated into the movement and was taught pyrotechnics and computer technology. By that time I had little memory remaining of my original family or my twin brother and I belonged completely to the tribe. I didn't think of Youssef again until I was assigned to replace him as part of our grand jihad against America."

I'd become so absorbed in his story that I was feeling relaxed, far more than reasonable for someone condemned to die. Then my vision began to blur. Hamzah's voice sounded far away, echoing as if it were coming from the far end of a long tunnel. I heard a hinge creak. The door opened and a woman stepped inside. Her image shimmered as if I were looking at her underwater. All I could make out was the dark skin of her arms and hands that extended toward me.

"Jamilah," I tried to say, but it was like trying to speak underwater. I imagined my voice reverberating through a liquid medium. Then the world faded once more from my awareness.

22

NINE MINUTES and 33 seconds. The countdown on the bottom screen of the Tesla had begun at fifteen minutes. I watched transfixed as the seconds ticked off. Beneath the timer was a message:

The bomb will explode when the timer reaches zero.

The bomb will explode if you place the car in gear.

The bomb will explode if you open a door or break a window.

The bomb will explode if you try to make a call or send a message.

"I'm finished," I thought. "There's no way out."

On the upper half of the screen was a map, showing my location, a parking garage a stone's throw from Boston's Hancock Tower.

"Is this real?" I thought, "Or am I dreaming or imagining it like so many other things? If I just close my eyes, will it all go away?"

I learned early in my psychiatric training that the suffering that people wreak upon themselves with their emotional symptoms often follows the Biblical law of "an eye for an eye." The punishment tends to fit the imagined crime. So it would make sense in the context of my survivor guilt that I might imagine myself about to be blown up. A fitting delusion. I could only hope.

The sound of the fan starting inside the Tesla startled me. I braced myself for the explosion, but if the engine had started, it would have been silent. I could feel the cool air flowing from the vent. The hairs on my arms stood up. All my senses were on high alert.

"I must be awake and this is real," I thought. "If only Jimmy was here to defuse the bomb." Jimmy, who still lay helpless in a hospital bed miles away, destined to survive his twin after all.

I took the safe road, the one more traveled. How did I ever wind up here?

*****

Four minutes and counting. Three minutes and fifty seconds, forty-nine, forty-eight.

The countdown stopped at three minutes forty-eight seconds. The lock screen on my phone lit up with a message: "Sit tight. Watch this screen."

Who sent the message? Were my captors just messing with me? Why would they do that if they were about to kill me anyway? I had no idea who else knew I was there or who else would have known about the bomb.

Three minutes forty-seven seconds. The countdown resumed. The bomber was back in control. My breath stopped short.

My phone lit up again: "Wait til the countdown stops again. Then open the door and run like hell for the stairwell to your left."

I breathed out, then took in a deep breath of stale air. "I'm still alive," I thought. "There's hope. Someone out there is looking out for me."

Two minutes...one minute...fifty-nine seconds, fifty-eight, fifty-seven, fifty-six.... I counted "one one thousand, two one thousand" under my breath as the timer sat at fifty-six seconds, then pulled the door handle.

The door swung open. I leaped out and sprinted for the stairwell. Suddenly people in space suits and dark-visored helmets poured out of the stairwell and from all directions. I dodged the torrent, glancing back as they converged on the Tesla, then disappeared into the stairwell and bounded down the stairs.

I'd been counting down in my head the whole time. By the time I reached the bottom, I was at five seconds and counting. I curled into a ball against the concrete wall and waited.

Three, two, one. A low rumble. The ground shook. Then silence. I was still alive.

A door slammed from above, then the clatter of footsteps running down the stairs. When I looked up, one of the space men was standing over me. I saw my reflection in the black visor of his helmet. A hand raised the visor to reveal the face of a woman, ethereal, an angel.

"Maybe I'm dead, after all," I thought.

"You OK, Dr. Tripler?" she asked. Her tone was no nonsense, earthly.

"I guess so. What happened up there?"

"The bomb squad contained the explosive. It detonated, but no one was hurt. I guess we got there in the nick of time."

"How'd you know where to find me?"

"An anonymous tip. Someone's been watching over you. Had it gone off a minute sooner, it would have taken down a city block. They were after the Tower."

"What happens now?"

"The FBI is looking for the terrorist cell that planted the bomb. We need to get you to a safe place."

An anonymous tip. And a highly skilled hacker who was able to hijack control of the Tesla's computer to disable the booby traps and delay the explosion long enough to rescue me. Friend or stranger? I could only guess.

"At least I get to live another day," I thought. "And at least for this moment, I'm not crazy. No voices. No delusions." What had just happened was terrifyingly real.

She led me outside to a waiting squad car and ushered me into the back seat, where I found myself next to another female officer who was holding something black in her lap.

"Sorry about this, Dr. Tripler," the second woman said as she raised the object, which turned out to be a hood, and placed it over my head. The hood had openings for my nose and mouth, but none for my eyes.

"I don't understand," I said. "You've just rescued me. I'm the victim. Why am I being treated like a criminal?"

"Just a precaution, Doctor. We're taking you to a witness safe house. It's essential to keep its location secret, even from the witnesses we protect. We're sparing you the handcuffs, but I'd advise you not to try to remove the blindfold."

We drove for a little over an hour. Halfway through the ride, the city sounds faded away and the car rolled quietly over smoothly paved roads. Then the tires rumbled over gravel for half a mile or so before the car came to a stop.

I was led, still hooded, for ten or twelve steps, then up a short flight of wooden stairs and through a door. We walked down a short hallway and crossed a threshold. The door closed behind me. I felt the edge of a chair against the back of my legs and a hand pushed gently down on my shoulder until I was seated. Then the hood came off.

I was in a dim, windowless, sparsely furnished room, seated in front of an empty table that was bolted to the floor. An empty chair faced me from the other side. Whoever saw me into the room withdrew and locked the door behind them. There was nothing left to do but wait.

After what seemed like an eternity, the lock clicked behind me. A paunchy, middle-aged man in a dark suit entered and took his place in the empty chair. He held a can of Coke in one hand. I could see the sweat on the can that told me that it had just come out of a refrigerator and was ice cold.

"Thirsty?" he said, pushing the can across the table.

"Parched," I replied. "Thanks." I grasped the can and prepared to open it, but discovered that it had already been opened and the tab removed. I hesitated a moment, then took a greedy draft of the cold, sweet liquid. Coke never tasted so good.

"Time to talk," the man said, "but first I need to tell you that you have the right to remain silent. Anything you say can and will be used against you in a court of law. You have a right to an attorney."

"Wait!" I screamed. "Why am I being Mirandaed? I'm the victim here. There must be some mistake."

"Then nobody's told you?" he said, appearing genuinely surprised. "You're under arrest for conspiracy to commit an act of terrorism. We have credible evidence that you were involved in an attempted bombing of a public building. And we found you in a car that was wired with explosives."

"But I was drugged and locked inside the car against my will. This is crazy. Do I look like a suicide bomber?"

"Stranger things have happened," said the man. "But we think you drove the car to the garage, then got double-crossed and locked in by your co-conspirators. You were lucky that a hacker managed to defeat the trap." He paused a moment. "So are you waiving your right to an attorney?"

"I didn't think I needed one."

"But it looks like you do. We've seen your posts on social media about your anger at the way your Lebanese girlfriend has been treated and your threats of vengeance."

"Wait. My girlfriend?"

"Yes. Jamilah Al Saud. I believe she's the widow of one of your patients. And it doesn't help that he died under mysterious circumstances."

"He committed suicide," I said, having never anticipated that that would be the least incriminating to me of all the possible ways he might have died.

"Perhaps, but we're not sure about that. We think you and his wife may have conspired to kill him. Once you've committed one crime, it's always easier to commit another."

This interrogation had already gone way too far. As absurd as the allegations seemed, I realized I'd need to defend myself.

"I want a lawyer," I said at last. "No more questions without one."

"Do you have a lawyer?" asked the man. "Or do we need to find you one?"

"I have a lawyer for my practice, but he's not a criminal attorney. I'll need to find one. But I'll need a phone."

"You must understand, Doctor, that you're a serious security risk. We can't let you have a phone. But we can provide you a list of criminal lawyers and the means to make a single call."

"What's going to happen to me now?"

"You will remain our guest, at least for a while, in this hideaway. We plan to keep your location secret until your arraignment. Then you'll be transferred to a secure prison." He paused to read my reaction.

"I wouldn't try to escape," he continued. "As unassuming as this house may seem, it's actually very secure. And if you were to find a way outside, you'd be amazed at the hazards that obstruct your path to freedom. Cooperation is your best bet to stay alive."

Having escaped what seemed like certain death, I was now equally screwed, accused of a heinous act of terror and of the murder of my patient, Youssef Al Saud. I had no idea what happened next. I'd heard of suspected domestic terrorists being flown to other countries to be interrogated in secret with torture that was outlawed in this country. Extreme rendition. There were books and movies about it.

The evidence was damning. My social media had been hacked and I'd been expertly framed for these crimes. Who could be responsible? And would I ever have the chance to prove my innocence?

23

TIME PASSED SLOWLY in the windowless room. It was hard to tell if it was day or night. I slept in fits and starts on the wooden floor. They brought me warm water and food, mostly stale bread and cheese. There was a sink in the corner of the room, bolted firmly to the wall, with a sliver of soap. My toilet was a five-gallon bucket that was swapped out when it got half full.

I awoke from one of my fitful dreams to popping sounds outside the room. I was instantly awake and on full alert. Footsteps followed, then the sound of a key in the lock. When the door swung open, someone rushed in and covered my head with another hood, plunging me into darkness, and pulled me roughly to my feet.

"Come with me. Hurry," said a young man in a stage whisper as he took me by the hand. I stumbled across the threshold into the hallway. After ten or twelve steps, my foot struck an obstruction and I tumbled forward, breaking my fall with my hands. The object that tripped me had some give, like a sack of flour, or perhaps a body. The man grabbed my hands and pulled me back to my feet. More popping sounds outside. Then silence.

"Keep moving. Just a little farther."

The solid floor gave way to the wooden stoop and the short flight of steps. Then a hand on top of my head guided me with pressure into the seat of a car. The car door slammed shut and the car began to roll across the gravel driveway.

"Where are you taking me now?" I asked. "I have a right to know where I'm going."

"Patience," came the response from the driver in the seat in front of me. A woman's voice. And a hint of a foreign accent.

"Who are you?" I demanded.

"Easy, friend," said the young man beside me. "We're the cavalry." When he spoke aloud, his accent was distinctly British.

"Then why am I still wearing this blindfold?"

"For your own protection. It's best that you can't tell anyone the location of the place we're taking you. That way, they can't beat it out of you if you fall again into the wrong hands."

We rolled over the smoothly paved secondary road back to the highway, took an exit a half hour or so later to another country road, then glided down an incline to a stop. I heard the whir of a garage door lowering behind us. Then the hood came off and the door opened to let me out.

As I stretched my legs, the driver's door opened and the driver got out and turned to face me. When I first saw her face, I thought for just a moment that I was looking at Jamilah. She had the same dark hair, dark complexion, and angular features characteristic of Semitic people, but her facial expressions and attitude were distinctly different. With Jamilah there was always a subtle undertone of flirtation that kept me in her spell. This woman had the bearing of a soldier: grim, intense, distant, untouchable. When she spoke, her syntax was perfect and her vocabulary and pronunciation suggested a strong British influence in her education, but her language was also tinged with an accent I'd heard before from a colleague during my training, an Israeli.

"Dr. Tripler," she said, holding out her right hand. "They call me Seleta." I shook her hand. Her grip was forceful and her gaze intense. There was no room for doubt who was in charge of this encounter. I still had no idea who these people were or why they'd taken me.

"Do I assume that I'm now your prisoner?"

"Prisoner? Hardly." A wisp of a smile passed her lips. "You were a prisoner when we found you. Consider yourself more our guest."

"But I'm not free to leave," I said.

"I'm afraid not, Doctor. At least not for now. We will need your cooperation if we are going to find the people who tried to bomb the Tower. Besides, by now your picture has been shown on every cable news station. You are a wanted man, presumably part of a terrorist cell. And there are more than a few of your countrymen who would be delighted to deliver vigilante justice."

"Isn't that what the people who were holding me were trying to do? Find the terrorists?"

"Yes, but they were on the wrong track. We know, at least, that you weren't in on the plot. You were an unfortunate bystander."

"Then why don't you work together?"

"Dr. Tripler," she said, "you can't understand the complexities of this business. Your people and ours don't always play nicely, and they were getting in our way. We needed you. You seem to be at the nexus of this affair. So we took you."

"The gunfire back there and the body on the floor. How many were killed?" I asked. The thought of more innocent bloodshed for my sake horrified me. It was enough that Joe and Kimi had already died.

"There were casualties," she acknowledged. "You're better off not knowing the details. You should understand, though, that the people imprisoning you came from the fringes of law enforcement. If you haven't already figured it out, they weren't nice people. I wouldn't lose much sleep over them."

I would definitely lose sleep over them in the nights to come. I didn't think much of the paunchy detective who'd interrogated me, but the thought of him lying in a pool of blood on the floor of the house made me nauseous. And what of the angel with the bomb squad who'd rescued me from the stairwell? I certainly hoped that she'd left the house after delivering me there and wasn't among the victims.

"Nexus," I thought. Somehow I'd gone from quietly practicing psychiatry to being at the center of a plot to blow up a building, and I'd gone stark raving crazy in the process. I had no idea whether I could trust these people any more than the last ones.

"Seleta," I said, "How do you expect me to help you find the terrorists?"

"You will help us connect the dots, starting with your patient who died in the river, then whatever you've learned about his wife, and the unfortunate disappearance of your other patient, Kimi Jones. How you wound up in the Tesla is somehow connected to how these pieces fit together. You were not chosen randomly, Doctor. Someone chose you to be the bearer of the bomb. That's the person we need to find."

Whoever these people were even knew about Kimi. But they apparently didn't know that she was murdered right before my eyes. That was one of the pieces of the puzzle that I still held and wasn't going to give up right away. Perhaps I could leverage it to pry loose one of the clues that they held. And perhaps that would eventually lead me back to Jamilah.

24

SELETA and her colleagues treated me well, far better than my previous captors. I concluded that they were indeed Israeli, most likely Mossad, the crack Israeli intelligence agency, and that they could likely be trusted to be on the right side of the struggle with the terrorists. They gave me a reprieve for the rest of the day to recover from my ordeal before engaging me in earnest the next morning in their interrogation. I decided it was in my best interest to cooperate as fully as possible, so our dialogue was more of a collaboration than a contest.

"Did you see any of the people who abducted you before the bombing attempt?" Seleta asked.

"I saw one of my captors clearly and caught a distant glimpse of another."

"Did you recognize anybody?"

"Yes. The man was the spitting image of my patient Joe. I learned that he was the identical twin that Joe believed had died when they were children. His given name was Ahmed, but they call him Hamzah now. He was quite free with me about his background because he apparently assumed that I wouldn't survive the bombing."

Seleta nodded. "Hamzah," she said. "That matches what we know. Our agents followed him to your country, but then lost track of him. We picked up the trail too late to prevent the terror attack. It was fortunate that someone hacked the Tesla at the last minute and averted disaster."

"Someone? Then you weren't the ones that created the hack?"

"Sadly no. We certainly tried. But despite our considerable skills we were unable to get into their system. Their security was very sophisticated and the system couldn't be entered without a digital key. It would have had to be done by an insider or someone who came into possession of the key."

My mind flashed to the tiny memory chip that Jamilah had slipped into my pocket and later reclaimed. The cipher she was trying to solve. Could the solution have been the digital key and had she managed to crack it? Then I flashed to the ephemeral figure at the end of the corridor in Hamzah's lair. Had that been Jamilah? And if so, was she confederate or intruder?

"He confessed to me that he'd murdered his brother," I said, returning to my narrative. "What a horrendous thing to do."

"Yes. The things that fanatics do in the interest of their cause no longer surprises me. We guessed that he'd killed his brother. And we believe that he'd earlier found a way to poison him."

"Poison? What do you mean?"

"To bring about his paranoia and hallucinations," Seleta said. "You must have gathered in your history that Youssef had no prior history of mental illness. It had come virtually out of the blue. Certainly not impossible, but in the light of subsequent events, a toxic psychosis makes the most sense."

"Toxic," I repeated, the wheels turning in my head. "If Joe's psychosis was the result of a toxin, then perhaps mine has been, too."

"Your psychosis?" Seleta seemed surprised. Perhaps this was one of the pieces they didn't already have. "What do you mean?"

"I've been hallucinating," I said, "at least some of the time. I began hearing voices around the time that Joe was killed and believed like he did that someone was trying to kill me. Of course, given what's happened to each of us, that might not have been delusional after all."

"Some of the time?"

"Yes. It went on for several days until I couldn't stand it any longer. It drove me from my home. I spent nearly a week in Maine on a farm off the grid. The hallucinations resolved spontaneously after the first couple of days. I was hearing voices again in the Tesla. That was after Hamzah drugged me."

"What did you and Joe have in common that might account for a toxin?"

"Beats me," I said, "except perhaps for Jamilah. But my hallucinations continued long after she disappeared."

"What can you tell me about her disappearance?" asked Seleta. She was now treading on ground that I'd considered avoiding. If we were to solve the puzzle, though, all the pieces would have to be on the table. My hand went to the wound on my forehead. The sutures had still not been removed and were becoming embedded in my flesh.

"There was an incident," I began. "It started when I spotted what I thought was Joe, but now realize must have been his brother. He led me to a carousel near the Boston waterfront, not far from the Market. Jamilah was there...and Kimi." Tears came to my eyes. I choked on my words and had to stop and regain my composure.

"As the carousel turned, each came into view and had a gun to her head. Joe...Hamzah said I must choose who would live and who would die." I was now sobbing. "It was agonizing." Seleta sat patiently until I was ready to resume my story.

"I chose Jamilah. It was a moment of impulse. I'm not even sure why I chose her. As Kimi disappeared around the other side, I heard a shot. When she came back into view, she was lying in a pool of blood."

"What happened then?"

"Hamzah had been holding me back from the carousel platform. As the carousel came around, Jamilah and her captor had vanished. He released me with a shove and my head struck the edge of the platform. Then the lights went out. I woke up in a hospital bed."

"And that was the last time you saw either of them? Jamilah or Kimi?"

"Yes. They both seemed to have vanished. I assumed that Kimi was dead. Who could survive a point-blank gunshot to the head? And I thought perhaps Jamilah was dead, too. That they had gone ahead and murdered her despite my choice. She never showed up at her home. And as far as I knew, there was nobody else in her life except me that would have missed her."

"Like Sophie's Choice," said Seleta, her face softening for the first time since we'd met. I knew exactly what she meant. She was referring to a movie about the Holocaust is which a woman was commanded by her Nazi captors to choose in an instant which of her two children would die and which would be spared. There was no right answer and her choice haunted her for the rest of her life.

"Is there anything else you can tell me about Jamilah," said Seleta after a respectful pause.

"Yes, there is," I said, ready to put everything on the table. "When Joe was admitted to the hospital, he had a computer that contained what seemed to be encrypted messages. He had no idea what they were or why they'd come to him. I guess they were meant for his brother, who hadn't yet taken his place."

"What happened to the messages?"

"Jamilah had his computer at their home overnight and downloaded the messages to a memory chip that she slipped into my pocket at the hospital and later took back. She claimed not to understand the contents, but surmised that part of it was a coded message and the other part an encryption key to decode the message. As far as I knew, she never solved it, unless…"

"Unless what?"

"Unless it contained the digital key to their system and she was the one who saved my life."

"That's an interesting theory," said Seleta, shaking her head, "but we have another idea about Jamilah Al Saud. We think that she might be Hamzah's confederate, his commander. We suspect that Jamilah is the mastermind behind the bombing."

I let Seleta's words sink in. My mind flashed again to the shadowy figure at the end of the corridor. I hadn't yet shared the details of what I'd seen with Seleta and considered telling her. It certainly looked bad for Jamilah. But I still hoped that Seleta was wrong and that Jamilah, if she was still alive, was working on the right side. That piece of the puzzle stayed with me.

25

I WAS HAVING breakfast the next morning with Seleta when I heard the door to the hideout open and footsteps coming toward us. It sounded like three or four people were headed our way. Then, in the door to the kitchen stood a person, head covered with a hood, as mine had been when I first came to this place, and hands bound together in front...brown, slender hands, a woman's hands.

I felt my heart skip and my breath stop. I looked at Seleta, whose face expressed that she knew what I was thinking. She gestured to the agent who now stood beside the hooded figure. He reached over and removed the hood.

"Jamilah," I shouted and sprang up from my chair. Seleta's arm shot out in front of my chest and pushed me back down. I stared, flooded with emotions, at Jamilah.

She barely looked like the exotic, commanding woman I remembered. Her face was covered in bruises. She'd been beaten and her head hung limply forward. Her hair was tangled and matted with blood. One eye was swollen shut. Her lips appeared almost too swollen to speak. As happy as I was to see her alive, I was devastated to see her so battered and defeated. And I was terrified of finding out whether or not Seleta was right about her.

Seleta gestured with her left thumb and the agent escorted Jamilah out of the room.

"We will clean her up and make her comfortable," said Seleta. "Then we will set about finding out who she is and what she knows."

"Do you mean torture?" I asked. "She already looks badly beaten. How much more can she take?"

"I have something different in mind," said Seleta. "I believe you have a saying about catching more flies with honey than with vinegar." She shot me a mischievous look.

"And…?"

"You, Dr. Tripler, will be the honey. You seem to have a connection with her, for better or for worse. She may still trust you. So we will arrange for you to have some time together and you will find out whatever you can."

"What makes you think she's the leader of the cell?" I asked.

"We know something of her history," said Seleta. "Jamilah was born in Lebanon and was raised in an area that became infiltrated by Hezbollah militia, the jihadist arm of Iran. When she was twelve, she suddenly showed up at the JFK airport and was claimed at the border by a family, who said she was their niece. She was released to them and finished growing up in their home. While she studied journalism at NYU, she met and subsequently married Youssef Al Saud, who was then a student at Columbia."

"How does that implicate her?"

"She may have been recruited by Hezbollah and sent to become part of a cell while embedding herself in our society. Her meeting with Youssef might have been random, but we think that she might have singled him out as Hamzah's twin brother as part of the larger plot. Perhaps you will be able to confirm our suspicions."

I sat on pins and needles for the next two days. Then, just before dawn, as I lay in my bed, still in the twilight state of sleep, I heard a light rapping on my door. I opened the door and Jamilah slid silently through the opening, then closed the door behind her. She placed a finger on my lips before I could speak.

"Someone left the door to my cell unlocked," she said. "I've been looking for you for the last hour. We need to speak before they discover me missing and come to find me." Jamilah looked much better than when I'd first laid eyes upon her. The bruises on her face were beginning to fade. Her eyes were both open and the swelling had gone down in her lips. Her hair was no longer tangled and was pulled tightly back from her face and tied behind.

I wanted desperately to embrace her and to comfort her, but remembered my mission and resisted the impulse. I had to stay objective. This was the meeting that Seleta had promised. Jamilah's door had been left deliberately open and breadcrumbs had been left leading her to my room.

"How are you, Zack?" she said, placing a palm gently on my cheek and looking into my eyes. This was the first time since I'd known her that she called me by my first name. It felt familiar, intimate. Was she truly happy to see me or was I being manipulated?

"OK, all things considered. At least I'm in one piece, except for this wound on my forehead. What about you?"

"I've been better. These people play rough. They think I'm in league with Youssef's brother and have been treating me like a dangerous enemy. I need to prove that I'm not. I need to prove it to you and then you need to convince them."

"They seem to have a lot of reasons to suspect you," I said, "starting with your origin in a Hezbollah infiltrated enclave. How do I know that you haven't been planted here to attack us?"

"Because somewhere in your soul, you believe in me." she said. "It's your profession to read people, and until now you've trusted me. I promise your trust has not been misplaced. Let me start by telling you the rest of my story."

We sat side by side on the edge of my bed. She placed a hand on mine and turned to look me in the eyes.

"I was born in southern Lebanon, where my family raised sheep on a small farm. I was twelve when the Hezbollah guerillas moved into the region surrounding our farm and began setting up rocket launchers throughout the countryside. One day, two of the fighters came to our door and demanded access to the house so that they could install one of their rockets inside."

I sat and listened attentively, imagining that she was one of my patients and we were sitting in my office in search of answers to her problems. Listening to details was one of my best honed skills.

"I watched my father argue with one of the men. When he raised his fist at him, the man struck him across the face with the butt of his rifle and knocked him to the floor. My father tried to get up, but the man struck him again with the blunt end of the stock and my father went limp. My mother, hearing the commotion, ran into the room and the other man grabbed her from behind while she flailed her arms and legs. I watched with horror while the first man drew his handgun and shot my mother in the head. He then turned back to my father, put the barrel of the gun against the middle of his forehead and fired."

Jamilah shuddered. I felt the wave travel down her arm to the hand that still sat on mine. I expected tears, but there were none. They must have long since dried up.

"I crept along the wall of my bedroom until I reached the open window and slipped out as quietly as I could. I flattened myself against the rear wall of the house. I could see the neighbors to the left of us peering out of their windows to see where the shots had come from, but they were too frightened to come outside. I heard the men inside ransacking the house to make sure there was nobody else there. They left as darkness was falling. It was getting cold fast. I crept back in the window to find some warm clothes, then out again through the window and into the countryside. The other villagers were so afraid that there was nobody I could trust to keep me safe. The bad men would figure out soon enough that I had survived their massacre and would comb the village for me." She paused to assess my reaction to what she was telling me, then continued her story.

"In the mountains at the edge of the village, I was at home. I knew the terrain for several miles around and had gained the high ground by daylight. In the valley beyond I could see the smoke rising from the houses in the next village, where my uncle and cousins lived. By the time I reached my uncle's house, I was parched and breathless. My hands and knees were scraped and bloody.

"My cousin Ali, who was 18, saw me first and I hushed him with a finger to my lips. He hid me in his room, and I sobbed as I told him how I'd watched my parents die just hours before. He didn't think it was a good idea for anyone else to know I was there and he promised to get me to safety. We traveled mostly by night from village to village until we reached the outskirts of Beirut where we found the home of an aunt who was a professor at University. She hid me, changed my identity, and found a family in the United States who claimed me as their niece and arranged passage to Syracuse, New York. I believe you already know the rest."

She waited again to assess the impact of her story. It had been powerful, as fraught as any of the stories of trauma to which I'd been witness in my practice.

"Then you were never under the influence of Hezbollah," I concluded.

"Never!" she replied. "I despised them and vowed to avenge the deaths of my parents. I've dedicated my life to avenging them. It's why I joined MI6 and that's how I've learned so much about ciphers."

Her story was convincing, but if she were indeed the leader of a terrorist cell, being convincing would be one of her skills. As much as I wanted to believe her story, I had no way to corroborate it.

"MI6," I repeated. "If you're British intelligence, why haven't you told Seleta?"

"I tried, but there was no reason for her to believe me." said Jamilah. "They had no prior knowledge of my existence. I worked in very deep cover. And I carried nothing to identify me. That's how we work. But," she paused for effect, "I can prove it to you."

There was a knock on the door.

"Are you OK, Dr. Tripler?" said a voice from outside. "Our prisoner is missing. We thought she might have come looking for you."

"I'm fine," I said. "I'll join Seleta for breakfast in just a few more minutes."

"Time is short," I said, turning back to Jamilah. "If you can prove it, now's the time."

"I'm the one who saved you from the bomb. I hacked the Tesla with the key I decoded from the memory chip and stopped the clock."

"And what's the proof that it was you?" I asked, feeling hopeful that her story was true.

"I stopped the clock twice," she said. "Do you remember the times?"

I did. They were indelible in my memory.

"The first time," she continued, "I stopped the clock at three minutes forty-eight seconds. The second time was at fifty-six seconds. Does that match what you remember."

"It does," I said, breathing a sigh of relief. Only the hacker would know the details of what occurred while the program was in the hacker's control. At least, that was what I believed, what I wanted desperately to believe.

Another knock on the door. This time the door opened from the outside. Two agents rushed in, grabbed Jamilah by the arms, and dragged her out.

"You know the truth now," she said as she slid across the threshold. "My life is once again in your hands."

26

I COULDN'T WAIT to tell Seleta what I'd learned. At breakfast, I told her that Jamilah was MI6, an agent on our side of the conflict, and shared the proof that she'd provided that should have exonerated her.

Seleta listened patiently. I tried to read her face, but her only reaction was a barely imperceptible shake of her head from side to side at the very end of my story.

"We will check out her story," she said, "but we're not ready to let her go until we're certain of who she is."

"What about the proof she gave me?"

"I understand how much you want to believe her. You must understand, however, how tenuous that proof is. It is conceivable that the people who planted the bomb were still able to observe what the hacker was doing to their program. These people are far too knowledgeable to have let the hacker lock them out entirely."

"What happens now?"

"She will be treated well, but will remain our captive for now. We'll reach out to MI6 for whatever they are willing to share about her."

"Can I see her again?"

"Patience, Dr. Tripler. All in time."

I was crestfallen. I desperately wanted to believe that Jamilah was on the right side of this conflict. The image of the woman at the end of the corridor behind Hamzah flashed back in my mind. I still hadn't shared that observation with Seleta, perhaps because I knew deep in my soul how damning it was.

The following hours crept by with no word from Seleta. Night fell. As I lay on my bed in pitch dark pining for sleep, I heard the click of a latch. My eyes had adapted to the dark enough to see the shadow of the door to my room swing open and the shadow of a figure stealing silently across the room. A hand was over my mouth before I could cry out.

"Shh," whispered a familiar voice in my ear. "It's time for us to get out of here."

I was once again faced with an instant choice with potentially disastrous consequences. Go with Jamilah and perhaps wind up back in the hands of the terrorists or cry out and risk putting an innocent woman back in harm's way. As before, I chose Jamilah.

She led me down the hallway toward the front entrance, past an obstacle course of fallen bodies. I counted three. My gut wrenched at the possibility of again being the cause of innocent blood being shed.

The door was already unlocked. A car was waiting outside with the rear door open. Jamilah tugged at my hand until we slid into the back seat and the door was closed. The car, an electric, started silently and moved onto the road. At least this time, there was no hood over my head and I could see where we were going.

"The bodies on the floor…?" I queried Jamilah.

"No worries," she replied. "We're all on the same side. They'll be out for a while longer, but nobody's been hurt in this operation."

I breathed a sigh of relief.

"As I told you, Zack, I work for MI6. These are my people. I brought you with me because I thought you'd be safer with me."

"Where are we going?"

"To our boat anchored off the coast of Gloucester. It's our local command post for the pursuit of the terrorists. We believe they're on another boat in the area."

The car rolled through Chelsea over the Mystic River Bridge and onto the coastal road north. We sat together, mostly in silence as questions shot through my mind.

"Thanks for choosing me...again," Jamilah said at last. "I understand how hard both decisions must have been."

"I thought they'd killed you, too, back at the carousel. How did you escape?"

"As you are aware by now, I'm a highly skilled operative. Subduing an assailant is routine. I'm sorry I had to disappear. You must have been very worried."

"I didn't know what to think. Being responsible for Kimi's death was burden enough."

"And there's that." Jamilah paused long enough to make full eye contact. "We have reason to believe that

Kimi's alive. She's been spotted by our surveillance on the terrorist's boat."

"Alive? How can that be? She was lying in a pool of blood."

"We don't know," said Jamilah. "She disappeared from the scene. Her assailants must have taken her with them."

I felt elated. For the second time that day I was relieved of the burden of responsibility for the deaths of others. Kimi's death had been personal, the result of my active choice, a burden of guilt from which I'd never expected to recover.

"Unfortunately, my dear Zack," Jamilah continued, "the presence of a hostage on board their boat will make our job considerably more difficult. We will do our best to spare her life."

The car reached its destination at the edge of a beach, now deserted in the dead of night. I stepped out of the car. The expanse of the sky was moonless and cloudless. The stars shimmered in the canopy above away from the intruding lights of the city.

We made our way to the edge of the water, where a zodiac skiff floated offshore. We waded until we were nearly chest deep and hoisted ourselves aboard. The motor started and the rubber boat took us out into the darkness. The cold night air and wind against my wet clothes chilled me to the bone. A quarter of an hour later, the outline of a yacht appeared against the horizon, shrouded in darkness except for a lantern pointed straight at us and flashing in a regular pattern.

Once on board, I was ushered into an interior compartment that was well lit. On the bed was a fresh set of clothes and on the floor a pair of Nikes.

"They're your size," said Jamilah from behind me. "We left in a bit of a hurry. I'm sorry you didn't have time to dress."

"Now what?"

"Now we find the enemy. We intend to capture the cell's commander."

"Hamzah," I said.

"Perhaps, but we don't think he's the leader."

"Then who is?"

"That, my dear Zack, is our next puzzle."

27

I AWOKE to the gentle rocking of the boat and the sounds of footsteps running on the deck above. There was a brief knock on my cabin door. Then the door cracked open. The sky, still dark, was obscured by dense mist. A young man peeked through the opening.

"Come with me, Dr. Tripler," he said in a crisp British accent. "We have the terrorists' yacht on our radar and are about to strike. We will be monitoring the raid via video feed. You can watch it unfold."

He led me to a compartment crammed with electronics, the command center of the boat. A large screen was mounted on a wall. The video feed was live, coming from head-mounted cameras on two of the agents, but there was little to see through the fog that was providing cover for the mission. As the pair of zodiacs pulled away from the boat, light began to filter from the horizon and Jamilah briefly came into view, dressed from head to toe in black and crouched tightly against the bottom of her vessel. The video rocked with the motion of the dinghies.

Suddenly, the target vessel loomed from the darkness. The rubber bows of the zodiacs made contact and the team of six scrambled over the gunwale, guns blazing. Three of the enemy fell in the initial assault. Others returned fire and one of Jamilah's comrades went down. Another round of gunfire and two more terrorists hit the deck. Then to my horror, the camera turned toward Jamilah, who was being held by a man with a gun to her head. I flashed back to the scene on the carousel. This time the outcome was out of my hands.

The sound of propellers came through the feed. The figure of a woman entered the screen, much of her face obscured with black grease, dangling by a rope from a helicopter, holding a rifle and closing in fast on the boat. She fired as she hit the deck. Jamilah's captor went down. The face of her savior flashed briefly on the screen, but too much of her face was obscured with grease to identify her.

The deck had been cleared. Jamilah and her rescuer harnessed her fallen comrade to the rope still dangling from the helicopter above. It rose and lifted him away.

Then from below appeared another man, one arm encircling a barefoot woman in a bandanna, the other holding a gun to her head. The camera zoomed in on Hamzah and the woman. Much of her face was covered by the scarf. I noticed first her dark hands and feet, then made out enough of her features to identify Kimi. He was shouting to the invaders to back off or he'd kill the hostage. I held my breath as Jamilah and her comrade not only held their ground, but calmly approached. I braced for the gunshot.

The blast from the gun was followed by a powerful spurt of bright red blood that soaked the bandanna and covered Kimi's face. The picture wobbled out of focus as the bearers of the cameras ran toward the pair. When the camera came back into focus, Hamzah's body lay motionless on the deck. Jamilah and the mystery woman flanked Kimi, who was still standing, covered in Hamzah's blood.

It was over. Hamzah and the rest of his crew lay dead. Kimi Jones was miraculously alive. My heart was still pounding from the raid and the suspense of the threats to Jamilah's and Kimi's lives. I felt a thrill from witnessing their narrow escapes and relief at last of my guilt for having condemned Kimi to death. While I felt little pity for the dead terrorists, I felt a twinge in my gut at seeing Joe's identical twin join his brother in death.

I watched as the assault team boarded the zodiacs to head back to their boat. The helicopter returned and scooped their commando from the deck of the ship. She waved to the others with her rifle as she departed.

Once the zodiacs were at a safe distance from the terrorists' yacht, they triggered the charges they'd planted. With a massive explosion, the boat sank from view.

I was waiting on deck for Jamilah and Kimi when they arrived on board. An agent hustled Kimi past me before I could make contact and took her below deck. Jamilah caught my eye and signaled me to let them go. I met Jamilah halfway across the deck and we embraced. It felt thrilling to have her in my arms. She released her hold first, but not before kissing me below my right ear, just like the first time we met. Something about this kiss felt more like a bookend than a beginning. I had a premonition that I might never see her again.

Jamilah found me again a couple of hours later. She'd had time to clean up and was back in civilian clothes.

"There's something you need to see," she said as she led me back into the command center with the screen.

Kimi sat at a table in another room across from an agent. She'd been cleaned up and her head was wrapped in a fresh scarf. It looked like she was being interrogated.

"I don't understand," I said. "What's going on?"

"Keep watching," she said and she whispered something into a microphone.

The agent walked around the table and unwrapped the head scarf. Kimi was scowling, but sat motionless as she allowed the scarf to be removed. I noticed that her hands were bound in her lap beneath the table. Then my hand went automatically to the healing wound on my forehead, still raw from my collision with the carousel.

The left side of Kimi's head bore no visible wound. The agent had her turn her head so I could see the other side. No wound.

My mind flashed back to the scene in Jamilah's kitchen the morning after I'd crashed at her home. Something about the kitchen had nagged at my attention that I hadn't been able to identify. That piece now fell into place. Among Joe's tea paraphernalia had been a small, inconspicuous porcelain vessel, a tea container, identical to the one that Kimi had given me.

Jamilah waited and watched me until she could see by my expression that I understood.

"She wasn't a hostage," I said.

"No. We realized that when we saw her. That's why we bet that Hamzah wouldn't kill her. Instead, he turned the gun on himself rather than be captured."

"I remembered seeing a porcelain container in your kitchen. It was identical to one that Kimi had given me that was filled with finely powdered tea. I drank it to help me sleep."

"Joe was also drinking the tea every night. He'd acquired it from a local tea shop that he frequented, one run by an Asian woman whom I never met."

"That's how we both were poisoned. It's how we became psychotic. Not from trauma and loss as I'd suspected nor from genetics."

"There's more," said Jamilah. "Hamzah wasn't their commander."

"Kimi was." I concluded, "which is why he wouldn't kill her."

"One of the reasons, anyway," Jamilah said. "She's agreed to cooperate. Our agent is about to take her confession. Would you like to listen?"

I nodded and she turned on the audio feed. Kimi was just beginning to speak.

"I am the granddaughter of Japanese Americans who were interned in your concentration camps during World War II. Their imprisonment left indelible scars on their psyches, which were passed down from generation to generation. I inherited the stain on their honor and their rage at the country that betrayed them. I buried my rage as a teenager, focusing my rebellion on my parents, but after my parents were killed in an accident, my rage against your country worked its way to the surface and I vowed someday getting revenge."

I'd already heard the first part of her story in my office, but was now hearing another face of it.

"I married Andrew Jones, a Westerner, shortly before my parents died," Kimi went on. "Two years into the marriage, I couldn't stand the lie any longer and left him, traveling to the Middle East where I met Hamzah, a radical Shia Muslim. In his presence, the strength of my otherness blossomed, and I joined with his righteous anger against the Western powers that have held me under their thumb. When the US began separating immigrant families and incarcerating children on its Southern border, my rage boiled over and I swore to get even. Hamzah was already involved in a terrorist plot and I willingly joined him."

That part of her story was entirely new. I wondered whether any of it might have come out had I not ended the session in which her story had begun. But she'd come to my office on the pretense of treatment for a feigned illness. She'd shown up soon after Joe had been admitted to my care in order to get close to me and to control my narrative in case I were to come into possession of the information that had prematurely been sent to Joe's computer.

"After he told me about his twin brother, I concocted the plot to poison his brother with an herb that would make him psychotic and make his death look like suicide when his body was eventually found so that Hamzah could replace him. At that point, I began to call the shots. His comrades back home unfortunately sent the codes before the switch could take place. And then the doctor got in the middle of everything."

So the delicate Asian flower who'd insisted on leaving shoes outside and starting sessions with tea ceremonies was a hardened terrorist and the mastermind of a plot to bomb the Hancock Tower. She'd led Joe and me to both believe we were crazy, reinforcing my madness by staging her own death before she disappeared. She was behind Joe's murder and had left me for dead in the car bomb that Jamilah had hacked to save my life.

Kimi concluded her story and was led from the room. The sound of propellers appeared in the distance and reached a crescendo as the helicopter hovered over the yacht. Jamilah and I went on deck to meet it.

A woman in black dangled from a ladder that hung from the copter. She alit on the deck.

"Seleta!" I exclaimed.

Another mystery solved. Seleta was the commando who saved Jamilah's life. They were on the same side of this fight, after all. It just took a while for everyone to realize it.

Kimi was brought up on deck, hands still bound. Seleta fastened her into a harness and they flew away as the ladder was retracted into the helicopter.

"What's going to happen to her?" I asked.

"That will be up to Mossad," said Jamilah. "Hamzah's cell was connected to Hezbollah. This fight now belongs to the Israelis. They'll determine her fate. Our mission is finished."

28

WHEN THE YACHT pulled into the harbor, a rental car was waiting to take me back home, along with my driver's license, a credit card and cash.

"What about the authorities?" I asked the agent who handed me the keys.

"No worries," he replied. "We've taken care of it. Your name has been cleared. You're no longer a hunted man."

I took a long deep breath of the fresh salt air. I was free. No more hiding from the police. No more hiding from Hamzah and his thugs. And no more hiding from the demons that had tormented me from within, the product of Kimi's poisoned tea. I made a mental note to have the tea analyzed when I got back to find out what had caused my psychosis.

Jamilah didn't see me off. Perhaps she felt we'd had enough closure with our embrace and the conclusion of the mystery that we'd solved together. I was disappointed, but accepted that if this dreadful chapter in my life was ending, I would have to leave all of it behind, including Jamilah. Our lives no longer had common ground. She had her work ahead of her and I had mine.

I wasn't in a hurry to get home. I hadn't eaten since early the day before and stopped for breakfast before getting on the highway. The salt air and the morning's adventure left me ravenous. I devoured a tall stack of pancakes with real maple syrup and some house cured bacon along with two leisurely cups of coffee, smiling as

I thought about Otis and his hospitality on the farm. Someday, I'd return to Camden and Otis's farm to thank him. I'd have a hell of a story for him and his family.

I drove over the Mystic River Bridge into Somerville. When I entered Cambridge, I took a detour past Jamilah's home and parked across the street. The house was dark. There was no vehicle in the driveway. I wondered whether she'd ever return.

When I got home and looked in the bathroom mirror, there was still some swelling around the sutures in my forehead that were long overdue for removal. I thought about going to an emergency room, but decided it would be simpler to remove them myself. I had a suture removal kit stashed away from the days of my medical training. I held each stitch with forceps and snipped the sutures close to the skin before pulling them through from the other end. The release of the tension on my skin provided immediate relief of the pain that I'd been too distracted until then to notice.

I took a couple of days to recover from my ordeal, but was eager to get back to work. I visited the hospital, but had no patients of my own on whom to round. My colleagues and the hospital staff were glad to see me. They had a slew of questions, having only recently read about me as a suspect in a terrorist bombing, but I waved them off for now. There would be time enough later to bring them up to speed.

Back at the office, I had a full schedule. Many of my loyal patients were eager to see me and to resume their treatment with me. I looked at the list. The first patient was marked as new, Ilsa Lund. Something was familiar about that name that I couldn't put my finger on.

I opened the door to my office. In walked a tall woman in a headscarf and sunglasses. As she walked past me, I noticed a faint whiff of a familiar scent that made my pulse quicken. When the glasses and scarf came off, Jamilah sat before me.

"I owed you a last goodbye," she said, "before going away forever. Jamilah Al Saud must disappear. I will have a new identity and a new mission somewhere distant from here. You've been a good partner in this mission, even if an unintentional one. And you were kind in my moment of grief when Joe died. I shall miss you, Zack."

"I'll miss you, too," I said, "more than you can imagine."

I still had so many questions. Not the least of them was how she wound up married to Joe. Had it been planned way in advance, somehow anticipating his role in the terrorists' scheme?

"You must be wondering why I married Joe," she said, as if reading my mind. "It was an accident. We were in school together, both studying computer engineering and coding. I fell in love with him. He seemed so calm and steady, while I struggled with the inner turmoil that arose from my violent origin. We were a good balance."

"Then when did you get recruited to British Intelligence?"

"Coding came naturally to me. My skills soon outstripped Joe's and I became fascinated with ciphers. Solving them was a game of which I never tired. My reputation came to the attention of MI6 and they found me a year and a half ago. When they offered me a role, I jumped at the opportunity to do some good in the world and perhaps also avenge my parents' deaths. When Joe died, solving his murder added to my zeal."

"You were impressive back there on the raid."

"MI6 trains their operatives well. Learning to fight was a new skill, very different from my role as a programmer, but I turned out to be a natural at that, too." She stood, wrapping her hair in the head scarf.

"We'll always have the Museum," she said, winking as she headed to the door and disappeared from my life forever.

The meaning of her pseudonym was suddenly clear. Ilsa Lund, Ingrid Bergman's character in Casablanca, a story of star-crossed lovers destined to part in the end in the interest of the greater good. Jamilah's poetic flair provided a fitting end to our story together.

About the Author

Rick Moskovitz is a Harvard educated psychiatrist who taught psychotherapy and spent nearly four decades listening to his patients tell their stories. After leaving practice, he in turn became a storyteller, writing science fiction that explores the psychological consequences of living in a world of expanding possibilities, including even the prospect of evading death. His Brink of Life Trilogy begins with the search for immortality in the mid-21st century and concludes with a search for the origin of human life.

In *Shared Madness*, he returns to his roots as a psychiatrist to write a first person tale of a psychiatrist who, while treating a psychotic patient, descends into madness and finds himself at the nexus of a deadly mystery.

www.ingramcontent.com/pod-product-compliance
Lightning Source LLC
Chambersburg PA
CBHW070922130626
46555CB00001B/247